HONEYSUCKLE ROSE

All in one day, Pennsylvania career woman Rose DeAngelo has broken her engagement to a man she doesn't love, wrecked her car and been fired from her job. Now she's in the front seat of a diesel truck headed for California with a man she suspects is behind the series of violent hijackings plaguing her clients. If only he weren't so attractive . . . Suspicion and passion are a potent combination. Stirred with danger and stoked with desire, the mix can be deadly — especially when you're falling in love with a killer . . .

Kate Douglas is a sucker for happy endings, but this romance author never makes it easy for her characters to find their own personal paradise. Kate's found hers in the wine country of northern California where she and her husband of almost thirty years live in an old farmhouse in the midst of a hillside vineyard.

When she's not writing, Kate does sports photography for many northern California cycling teams.

Visit Kate's Web site at:
http://www.katedouglas.com

KATE DOUGLAS

HONEYSUCKLE ROSE

Complete and Unabridged

ULVERSCROFT
Leicester

First published in 2001 in
The United States of America

First Large Print Edition
published 2003

The moral right of the author has been asserted

All characters in this book have no existence outside
the imagination of the author, and have no relation
whatever to anyone bearing the same name or names.
These characters are not even distantly inspired by
any individual known or unknown to the author, and
all incidents are pure invention.

British Library CIP Data

Douglas, Kate
    Honeysuckle Rose.—Large print ed.—
    Ulverscroft large print series: romance
    1. Love stories
    2. Large type books
    I. Title
    813.5'4 [F]

    ISBN 0–7089–4842–1

Published by
F. A. Thorpe (Publishing)
Anstey, Leicestershire

Set by Words & Graphics Ltd.
Anstey, Leicestershire
Printed and bound in Great Britain by
T. J. International Ltd., Padstow, Cornwall

This book is printed on acid-free paper

To my husband,
who has always encouraged my dreams.
I can never thank you enough.
And to Kathy Awe,
critique partner extraordinaire,
for caring enough to tell me when I've
written something really, REALLY awful!

1

Monday morning, Pittsburgh

'I know, Mr. Hannibal. Please, you must understand why we have to add a five percent risk premium to your usual rate . . . Mr. Hannibal, there's no need to be rude. Acme Insurance has paid out a substantial amount . . . I realize those thefts were unusual . . . yes, Mr. Hannibal, I agree, otherwise you . . . I understand you're upset, Mr. Hannibal. As I said, I agree, you do have an excellent record.'

Rose DeAngelo arched her back and ran tense fingers through her heavy twist of dark hair. It didn't help a bit. *Blast it!* Headaches like this one generally didn't start until *after* lunch.

A second light on the phone flashed. Rose stared at the little orange square, peripherally aware that it blinked in perfect time with the pounding in her head.

'Mr. Hannibal.' Rose clenched her teeth against the blossoming pain in her skull. 'There is no other option. I'm sorry. I'm going to switch you back to my secretary. You'll pay the additional five percent? Fine.

Please give Denise the route information.'

Rose took the next call, groaning audibly the moment she recognized the patronizing voice. Sighing, she reached into her drawer for two aspirin. James Dearborn was the last person she wanted to talk to right now.

Not a promising sign, Rose. She ignored the quiet voice in the back of her mind. Now was not a good time for analyzing relationships. Rose gulped the aspirin with a swallow of tepid coffee and grimaced at the bitter taste.

'James . . . hello.' She twisted the large marquis-cut diamond on her left hand. Why was it, lately, all her conversations with James made her ring finger itch?

'Please, James. I don't have time to discuss this right now.' Rose glanced through the glassed wall of her office into the waiting room beyond. Her boss leaned over Denise's desk, waving a large stack of folders under the young woman's nose.

'You want to what?' Line two blinked hypnotically. Line three quickly joined in. She couldn't possibly have heard James right. *What did he say? Set a date?* Rose furiously scratched the raw skin under the offending ring. 'No,' she said, well aware of the sense of desperation in her voice. 'I absolutely refuse to plan my wedding because your mother has a free weekend in July! No James . . . absolutely not . . . no, we can't discuss it at lunch with your mother. I don't have time for lunch today . . . are you giving me an ultimatum?' Rose pulled the ring off her finger, scratching frantically.

Denise, precariously balancing a huge armload of folders, opened the office door with her shoulder. Frank Bonner, the company president, glared through the open door into Rose's office, then rudely signaled for her to join him in his. James's voice droned on, bouncing around inside Rose's head, thumping in time to the pounding behind her eyes.

Denise set the pile of folders on the corner of Rose's desk, then quickly backed out of the office. As she closed the door the stack gradually slipped to one side. Rose stretched full length across the large oak desk, holding the phone to her ear with one hand, grabbing for the top of the pile with the other. She felt the snag in her new black stockings open up then run the length of her leg, crawling up her inner thigh at precisely the same rate of speed as the folders slid to the floor.

'We'll have to talk another time, James.' Rose took a deep breath and broke the connection. She knew she'd hear about her behavior later, but there was no way she could deal with him now.

She signaled for Denise to take the call on line three, then punched the button for line two. James's mother. Could this day possibly get any worse?

Alicia Dearborn's shrill voice crackled into Rose's ear. 'No, Alicia. I can't go to lunch with you and James . . . I'm sorry too. I'll have to call you back.' Rose gritted her teeth. 'I'm very busy. No, nothing special. Just a typical Monday. Good bye.'

Sighing, Rose replaced the handset. She stared at it a moment, daring the phone to ring, then picked the scattered folders up off the floor and piled them on her desk.

She couldn't put off her meeting with Bonner any longer, no matter how unpleasant the prospect. It had to be about the recent hijackings. Acme Insurance had paid a bundle in settlements the past few months and pressure around the office had been steadily building.

Most of that pressure had come from Rose's office.

Insuring special loads for long-haul trucking companies had its risks, but lately it appeared as if someone had it in for her clients. Even Hannibal Trucking's perfect record had been compromised with two major thefts in the past two weeks.

4

Rose glanced at the heavy oak nameplate on her desk, the one Mr. Bonner had presented to her the day he'd promoted her to manager. 'It'll make a dandy bookend,' she muttered. She stared at the etched letters of her name a moment longer, then headed out the door for the inevitable dressing down from the boss.

'Ms. DeAngelo.' Denise held up a stack of notes to catch her attention. 'That last call was from your Aunt Rosa. She left you a message, said you must be really busy since she was on hold so long.' Denise flipped through the notes, then held one out to Rose.

'I wish I'd known it was her.' Rose took the slip of paper. 'She's a lot more fun to talk to than James's mother.'

Denise laughed, then shrugged her shoulders philosophically as the phone rang again. She turned to answer it.

Rose unfolded the note, suddenly aware of a lump in her throat. She hadn't talked to Aunt Rosa for over a week.

Please tell Rose the honeysuckle's blooming. And tell her I love her. She's working too hard. Rosa DeAngelo.

The honeysuckle's blooming and I haven't seen Aunt Rosa in two years. The sweet scent of honeysuckle filled Rose's mind, the memory of the massive vine covering the porch at her aunt's bed and breakfast inn out in California a balm to headaches, frustrating clients, angry bosses and disappointing fiancés.

Rose looked through the window into Frank Bonner's office. He paced back and forth and gestured violently as he argued with someone over the phone, his angry words muted behind the soundproof glass.

Denise answered her phone again, at the same time indicating to Rose she had a call waiting. Rose ignored the blinking light, mesmerized by the ugly shape of Frank Bonner's mouth twisted in anger, visible but silent behind the glass.

She took a deep breath in a vain attempt to ease the tension in her neck and shoulders, then turned around to take the call in her office. As if mocking Rose, the marquis diamond twinkled at her from its resting place in the paper clip bowl. She picked it up, staring absentmindedly into its icy blue depths before answering the phone.

The door to the outer office opened. Rose paused with her hand over the headset and looked up to see James guiding his mother through the tastefully decorated foyer.

'Why me, God?' she muttered. How had the two of them gotten here so quickly? Lunch was beginning to look like a setup, with wedding plans as the main course.

She knew better than to think Alicia would ever take no for an answer. Or James, either, for that matter.

Why should he? He was just like his mother.

In fact, Rose had never noticed before how much the two of them resembled one another. Not a flattering observation at all since she thought Alicia Dearborn looked exactly like the ugly little Pekinese tucked firmly under the woman's left arm.

Suddenly it all fell into place: the rhythmic pounding in Rose's head, Alicia Dearborn's strident voice, James's placating tones, even Frank Bonner's flailing arms as he carried on his argument via speakerphone in his spacious, soundproof office across the hall.

Then it all drifted away as, once again, the sweet memory of honeysuckle filled Rose. Drawing a deep breath, she inhaled the peaceful, calming scent of her childhood, not the antiseptic, filtered air of her Acme Insurance Company office. Aunt Rosa was absolutely right. She *was* working too hard.

Rose drew her hand back from the telephone and all its blinking lights, picked up her heavy leather purse, slung her raincoat over her arm and quietly walked out of her office. She closed the door behind her and

7

straightened her shoulders at the solid sounding 'click' as the latch caught and locked her chaotic morning behind her.

Ignoring Alicia's imperious command that she explain herself, Rose smiled calmly at her secretary. 'Hold my calls, Denise. I've decided to take the afternoon off.'

'Well. It's about time you came to your senses, Rose. I'm glad you've decided to join Mother and me for lunch. We have to talk.'

Rose turned to James. Why, when she looked into the eyes of the man she'd promised to spend her life with, did she feel nothing stronger than regret?

'You misunderstand, James. I'm taking the afternoon off by myself.' She fumbled for the right words, finally deciding honesty was best. 'Please, I'd like for you to take this back.' She held the heavy gold and diamond ring out to him. 'We both know it's never going to work. We've known it all along.'

He didn't move. She looked at his face, searching for whatever had made her think she loved him. She'd once been so enamored of his dark blond hair and finely chiseled jaw, in awe of his elegant manners and cultured speech. But the man she thought she loved didn't exist at all.

I imagined you. The thought struck like a

bolt of lightning. *Am I that desperate?* Self awareness brought a sad smile to Rose's lips, followed by a sudden urge to giggle. James and his mother, her secretary Denise, even that disgusting little Pekinese, all stared at her with their mouths open!

Finally, a way to silence Alicia Dearborn. Feeling almost giddy with power, Rose tucked the ring into the breast pocket of James's custom tailored Armani suit, then quietly left the building. It didn't even bother her that James hadn't asked her to stay, hadn't reached out to her, hadn't disagreed with her. No, it didn't bother her at all.

Somewhere, a peaceful country road beckoned.

★ ★ ★

Rose wasn't certain how long she'd been driving, or how far. The isolated landscape loomed dark and unfamiliar, the heavy clouds were no longer visible in the night sky, and her trusty little Volvo had developed an unhealthy klunking noise.

She searched the horizon for the lights of Pittsburgh, but no telltale glow marked the sky. In fact, she hadn't seen any light other than the occasional flash of lightning for at least an hour. Rose glanced at the fuel guage.

9

Less than a quarter of a tank left.

At least her headache was gone. 'Along with my job,' she muttered as the first fat drops of rain splatted against the windshield. *Just what I need*, Rose thought, straining to see through the sudden downpour. *More proof that my life is totally out of control.*

'Well, not completely,' she amended. Stuffing that ugly ring in James's pocket had been rather empowering. Doing it in front of her secretary, the company president, and her once future now ex-future mother-in-law hadn't been bad, either.

'One of your better exits, Rose.'

She waited for the fully expected sense of guilt to swamp her, the feeling that, once again, she'd done something terribly wrong, but the only feeling Rose felt was *right*. Wrong would have been staying with James, going through with a loveless marriage. No, she thought, her decision to return that ugly ring and leave had been a long time coming.

She grabbed a clean tissue to wipe the condensation from the windshield and grinned. Too bad Aunt Rosa had to miss it. She loved dramatic exits.

Rose glanced down at her left hand, barely visible in the pale glow from the dash lights. It looked much better without the heavy diamond. She'd hated that ring from the

10

moment James put it on her hand, hated the sense of ownership James assumed once they'd become engaged.

To think she'd almost convinced herself she loved him. A sudden wave of loneliness swept over her and a hollow pain filled the pit of her stomach, reminding Rose why she'd agreed to marry a man she didn't love. Life was pretty empty for a thirty-year-old woman who lived alone and worked a sixty hour week.

She didn't even own a damned cat.

The tears Rose had been fighting all afternoon suddenly broke free. She fumbled in her handbag for another tissue, wiped her streaming eyes with one hand and guided the car through the growing storm with the other.

She didn't even like cats, for crying out loud!

'God, if you're there, can you tell me what to do?' she pleaded. 'Please, give me a sign!'

An ominous roll of thunder eclipsed the sputtering, coughing engine. Lightning flashed. A tree exploded, ahead and to the right. Cascading flames burst through the air as the huge pine toppled onto the road.

Screaming, Rose hit the brakes. The little Volvo careened sideways on wet pavement, spinning, slipping out of control, sliding and skidding through water and fiery embers until it stopped, trapped solidly among the flaming branches.

Rose screamed again and again until the rich scent of honeysuckle clouded her mind and a cloak of black velvet covered her eyes.

★ ★ ★

Mike Ramsey pulled the diesel truck with its heavily loaded trailer out of the yard at Hannibal Trucking and headed west. He checked his map and immediately took an exit on to a slower, alternate route. No point in making it too tough for the hijackers.

The headlights reflected off big, fat raindrops and an occasional flash of lightning arced between the clouds. Puddles filled low spots along the two-lane road, deep enough to catch the tires of the heavily laden truck. The rig bucked and swerved through one particularly large pothole. Ramsey shut the radio off to concentrate on his driving.

He hadn't hauled a load in years, not since he'd worked summers for his step-dad, but the knowledge he'd gained under Handy's patient tutelage had paid off more than once. Ramsey thought of the journey ahead and silently thanked the old man. This time the lessons could mean the difference between life and death.

Hijacking expensive loads off the nation's highways was big business, modern day piracy as bloodthirsty and brutal as any violent crime. How ironic, Ramsey mused, that after years of undercover work handling investigations for the Department of Transportation, he would find himself back in one of his step-dad's familiar rigs, hauling a load from Pennsylvania to California. Just the way it had been almost fifteen years ago, back when he was a struggling college student.

Except the purpose this time was two-fold.

Deliver the load, intact and on time.

And catch the hijackers before they put Handy Hannibal and a lot of other independent truckers out of business for good.

Hannibal Trucking had been hit twice in less than two weeks. Another theft could put the business under, especially if that damned insurance company put up a stink. Ramsey almost wished they would, because as far as he was concerned, Acme Insurance was part of the problem, if not all of it. Hannibal Trucking hadn't been the only company hit with the recent string of thefts. Ramsey'd talked to the other victims. All of them had two things in common. They'd all been insured by Acme Insurance, and they had all dealt with the same agent.

Ms. Rose DeAngelo.

Described by Handy as one extremely formidable woman. A real 'bitch on wheels,' in Handy's eloquent vernacular.

There had to be a connection. Everything Ramsey'd learned about the woman piqued his suspicions. Barely thirty years old, she was the only female division manager at Acme, a typical 'good old boys' operation. Never married but currently engaged to the son of one of Pittsburgh's wealthiest families, obviously an opportunist, both socially and professionally.

'Somehow, Ms. DeAngelo . . . ' His words trailed off and Ramsey grinned, enjoying the chase, sensing victory. He hadn't had a hunch this strong in ages, especially one so strongly supported by fact.

After reading the reports, he'd been surprised no one else had spotted the obvious. Only Acme's division manager had access to the routes, the shipping dates, the value of the goods on board. Not surprisingly, the thefts had started right around the time Rose DeAngelo got her promotion.

And I imagine they'll end about the time I slap the handcuffs on her. Grinning, he checked the rearview mirror.

She'd want this load. Her gang hadn't missed an expensive piece of heavy equipment in the last two months. The scraper lashed securely to the trailer behind Ramsey's truck was worth a small fortune. When the hijackers hit, Ramsey'd be waiting for them. When they started to talk, as crooks always did, Ramsey suspected they'd lead him directly to Ms. DeAngelo.

Then maybe he'd be able to cancel out some of the debt he owed Handy. When the DOT supervisor brought the case to Ramsey's attention, his first reaction had been anger. Why hadn't Handy asked for his help? Once he calmed down, Ramsey realized Handy'd acted true to form, just like the tough little bantam rooster he'd always been.

A little bantam rooster with a big heart of gold.

It felt good to know he finally had a chance to pay back some of the kindness Handy had shown him and his mother over the years. No other man had been willing to take on a hellraiser like Mike Ramsey, twelve years old and so full of himself even his mom had given up.

Then Handy came along. He swept Rebecca Ramsey off her feet and Mike Ramsey under his wing.

Ramsey smiled, remembering, then immediately sobered as a huge gust of wind buffeted the diesel. Rain formed a shimmering band of silver in the headlights and

15

lightning flashed again, closer this time.

Suddenly, just ahead, a huge pine tree burst into flame. Ramsey hit the brakes and down-shifted as the blazing tree twisted and fell, casting a shower of flame and sparks across the highway.

Stopping almost seventy tons of metal on a partially flooded road without jackknifing the rig took all Ramsey's skill and then some. Heart pounding, hands sweating, he fought the steering wheel and prayed.

The big diesel and its heavy load slid crossways on the narrow road, then shuddered to a stop. That's when Ramsey saw the car, a small, square sedan skidding broadside on the wet pavement, sliding toward him, toward the inferno of flaming pitch and burning wood that blocked the way between them.

★ ★ ★

They're never coming back, are they, Aunt Rosa?

No dear. They're not. There were no survivors.

How can we bury them, if the plane went down at sea?

We can't sweetheart. But we can always remember them.

*How? How, Aunt Rosa? I want them back.
I want Mommy and Daddy back!*

*I know Rose. I want them back too
. . . but, some things just can't be changed.
I'm sorry.*

What will happen to me?

*You'll stay here, sweetheart. You'll be my
little girl. I've always wanted a little girl of my
own, you know.*

I love you, Aunt Rosa.

*I love you, too, Rose. Now, will you help
me plant this?*

What is it?

*It's a honeysuckle vine. Your daddy always
loved honeysuckle, even when we were
children.*

Why are we planting it now, Aunt Rosa?

*To help us remember, sweetheart. To help
us remember.*

★ ★ ★

'Hold that light steady. Thanks. Was she
conscious when you pulled her free?'

'I'm not sure. I don't think so. I just
wanted to get her out before the car blew up.
How'd you guys get here so fast?'

'A neighbor called when he heard the
explosion. The fire station's just down the
road. She doesn't appear to have any serious

17

injuries. Just that bump on the head. She's damned lucky you showed up when you did.'

'I saw it happen. Almost didn't get my rig stopped in time. Hey, looks like she's coming around.'

The sweet scent of honeysuckle disappeared in the acrid stink of melted rubber burning Rose's eyes and throat. She coughed and blinked and tried to focus on the faces hovering just within her line of vision. The features were indistinct, lit from behind by an orange glow that flickered through the steady mist.

At least the driving rain had stopped.

'Wha . . . what happened?' Her voice sounded alien to her, a tortured whisper scraping raw throat tissue. 'Who are . . . ?'

'Mike Ramsey. I pulled you out of your car. Bill here's a paramedic.'

'Paramedic? I'm not hurt . . . am I?' Rose struggled to sit up. She managed to prop herself on her elbows, the better to see the two men squatting beside her.

'Doesn't look like it, thanks to Mr. Ramsey here.'

Rose squinted, bringing her savior's face into focus. The harsh glare of the emergency lights cast his features into deep shadow. She made out a high forehead, long, slightly crooked nose, dark eyes and brows, all framed

18

in thick, dark hair slicked wetly back from his face. A black smudge that could have been a burn crossed his right cheek, disappearing into the day's growth of beard covering his lean jaw. Still disoriented, her perusal took on a dreamlike quality as she stared at the slightly imperfect but attractive face with the shadowed eyes.

Eyes watching her just as intently. Intrigued, Rose forced herself to look away, beyond the fascinating Mr. Ramsey, at the smoldering heap of metal that had recently been her Volvo. She shuddered, and quickly turned her head. She could have died, would have died, but for this stranger.

'Thank you doesn't quite seem adequate, Mr. Ramsey.' Rose cleared her throat, then broke into a fit of coughing. The paramedic helped ease her into a sitting position. Ramsey knelt at her other side, sliding a strong, warm arm around her shoulders. Rose struggled to catch her breath, soothed by the gentle pressure of Ramsey's touch. It would be so easy to turn her face against his solid shoulder, close her eyes and pretend this Monday had never happened.

A sudden weariness overwhelmed her, weighing her eyelids, lulling her into somnolence. Only vaguely aware of the paramedic's gentle probing near her hairline, she was exquisitely conscious of the strong arm bracing her shoulders, the heat of the man's body so close beside her own.

A high-pitched tone shattered the moment. Ramsey's hand tightened protectively around Rose. She blinked her eyes open in surprise, just in time to see the paramedic sheepishly gesture to the radio clipped to his belt.

'Danged thing always scares the devil outta me when it goes off,' he muttered, holding the radio to his ear as he stood up and moved to one side.

Ramsey rubbed his hand lightly across the woman's back, aware of her trembling beneath his touch. Hell, his own hands were still shaking, the adrenaline coursing wildly through his veins. A few seconds later and he might not have saved her. He couldn't look at the burning wreck, didn't want to imagine this beautiful woman meeting such a horrible death.

She was a looker, even covered in soot and smelling slightly of burnt rubber and plastic. She felt good, too, pressed warmly against him, snuggled trustingly into the curve of his arm as if she'd been designed specifically to occupy that position.

Dream on, Ramsey. He jerked himself back to reality as he studied the woman in his arms. She looked shaken and vulnerable and oddly familiar. How could that be? She certainly didn't seem to know him.

Soot covered her face and a large bruise marred the left side of her forehead. Her dark hair fell partially undone, tumbling wildly around her shoulders.

She took a deep breath and her ribs expanded within his embrace. Ramsey focused on the tip of her tongue as it swept across her slightly parted lips.

'I really don't know how to thank you.' She sounded confused, uncertain. Bewildered. 'You saved my life.'

She swallowed. Ramsey watched the muscles in her throat contract. 'Seeing you're okay is thanks enough,' he answered, swallowing just as deeply. 'Miss, uh . . . ?'

'DeAngelo. Rose DeAngelo.' Her voice, a smoky whisper, teased his senses.

But . . . Rose DeAngelo? *No way!* This beautiful, vulnerable woman couldn't possibly be the 'bitch on wheels' Handy'd warned him about, not this wounded creature with soulful green eyes and trembling lips. This was his chief suspect? Ramsey thought of the file photo he'd seen, of the austere woman with the dark hair pulled tightly back from an unsmiling face and shook his head in mute denial of the improbability of the situation. Just as

21

quickly he wiped the expression from his face.

He'd had a life filled with coincidence and good fortune. He accepted it, knew it made him a successful investigator. He'd be a fool to deny coincidence. If this were the same Rose DeAngelo, opportunity lay, literally, within his grasp.

'Can you help me stand up, please?' She leaned forward, away from his support, out of his embrace, and held her hand out to him. Ramsey focused on the pronounced tremor in her long fingers.

'Are you sure?' He looked to Bill for confirmation. The paramedic ignored him, focusing intently on the voice crackling over his radio. 'Well, if you think you're okay.' Ramsey stood up and reached for her outstretched hand.

She grasped his hand and rose to her feet lightly, with the grace of a dancer. A smudged and rumpled dancer. She was tall, maybe five ten. Ramsey hadn't noticed before, not when pulling her out of the burning car had been his only concern.

'Ma'am, do you think you'll be okay?' Bill suddenly asked, grabbing for his medical bag. 'There's been a terrible wreck on the interstate, fifty or more vehicles, serious injuries. You should probably be checked out

22

by a physician, but . . . '

'Please, go ahead. I'm not hurt. Oh. Wait! My car . . . '

'I can take Ms. DeAngelo into town,' Ramsey offered. 'That is, if it's okay with you,' he added, looking not at her face but instead at their hands, still tightly linked. Her fingers trembled in his grasp.

He trusted his hunches. She was his primary suspect. He didn't want to feel sympathy for her. He certainly didn't need this attraction. Ramsey loosened his grip on her fingers and stuck both hands in his back pockets.

'You sure you don't mind givin' the lady a ride?' Bill gathered his equipment as he talked. 'The chief's called a tow truck. The county crew's on their way to clear the tree out of the road. Thanks Ramsey. Glad you're okay, Ma'am,' he added, tipping his cap and climbing into the ambulance.

The siren wailed, the lights flashed and the engine howled as the ambulance sped into the night.

Rose appeared stunned by the abrupt departure. She turned in Ramsey's direction, her eyes wide and frightened, and wrapped both arms around herself in a protective gesture.

Ramsey glimpsed a distant flash of lightning reflected in her deep green eyes and wondered just what he'd gotten himself into.

2

'I really do have to get back to Pittsburgh.'
Rose shivered, either from shock or the damp
air. She wasn't certain. Fear, maybe?
Uncomfortably aware of their isolation, her
gaze followed the red flashing lights as the
emergency vehicles raced away through the
chilling mist.

A single volunteer firefighter remained to
keep flares lighted at the accident scene, but
Rose felt very much alone with the intriguing
Mr. Ramsey. For all she knew, he could be an
axe murderer. A *heroic* axe murderer, but
still . . .

'No problem.' His words tickled her ear
and Rose jumped. *How'd he get so close?* She
stepped back.

'There's a little town just up the road,' he
said. 'You can call someone to pick you up.
Oh, almost forgot. Here's your bag. I grabbed
it when I grabbed you.'

'You saved my purse? I don't believe it!'
Rose laughed, suddenly more at ease as she
took the heavy black leather bag he held out
to her. An axe murderer would never risk his
life to save a woman's purse! 'You really are a

hero,' she said. 'Men never think of purses.'

'They do when they grow up with three sisters.' With one hand lightly grasping her elbow, Ramsey guided Rose toward a large tractor trailer rig parked at an angle on the far side of the fallen tree.

'Hannibal Trucking,' Rose read aloud. 'You work for Handy Hannibal?' Some of her tension eased. Handy was a respectable businessman. A pain in the rear to deal with, but respectable. He wouldn't hire an axe murderer.

'Sure do. You know Handy?' Ramsey opened the door and helped Rose climb the steps into the cab. She tried to hold her short skirt down but finally gave up, scrambling up the narrow step and over the fuel tank.

'He's one of my clients,' she said. 'I work for Acme Insurance, out of Pittsburgh.'

'Rose DeAngelo . . . Yeah, now that I think of it, Handy's mentioned you.' He laughed, a low, reassuring chuckle. 'As I recall, he referred to you as a pain in the ass, or something equally complimentary.'

Rose rolled her eyes and smiled back. 'You obviously know the same Handy Hannibal I know.' Unaccountably relieved, Rose scooted across the wide bench seat to the passenger side. It wasn't as if she were climbing into a truck with a perfect stranger, not when they both knew the same irascible old man. As ornery as Handy Hannibal was, Rose knew him to be honorable to a fault and his drivers all had excellent reputations. She tried to recall if he'd ever mentioned an employee named Mike Ramsey.

The name sounded oddly familiar but she couldn't place it. Handy talked about all his drivers as if they were his children. He must have mentioned Ramsey to her at some point.

Ramsey shoved a couple of maps aside and settled in behind the wheel. 'Here, I've got a cellular phone, if there's anyone you want to call.'

Rose looked at the phone. Normally she would have called James, but that seemed like a pretty tacky thing to do, especially after the way she'd broken their engagement. Her secretary, Denise, would be at home fixing dinner for her husband and two children. She couldn't call Frank Bonner since he'd probably fired her, and the demanding hours of her job had kept her from any social life that included friends.

Everyone had more important things to do than drive an hour through the stormy night to give Rose a ride home. Everyone except Aunt Rosa, but she was on the other side of the country. Rose's eyes filled with tears. 'No,' she whispered. 'No, I don't need the phone.'

Ramsey quietly studied her face, his dark eyes hooded and thoughtful. Rose took a deep breath and matched his intense gaze. 'Do you think I can rent a car where we're going?' she asked, almost afraid to acknowledge the idea that suddenly dominated her thoughts.

Ramsey blinked, then grinned. 'I have no idea, Ms. DeAngelo. But I do know where to get a decent meal. I don't know about you, but I'm starved. Rescuing damsels in distress has made me a hungry man. If it's all right with you, Madam Damsel, let's see if we can get this rig around that pine tree.'

★　★　★

The storm had returned with a vengeance by the time Ramsey pulled the huge tractor-trailer rig into the parking lot of a small restaurant on the outskirts of an even smaller town. He helped Rose climb down out of the cab and the two of them raced across the flooded lot through the churning downpour. Ramsey held his coat across Rose's shoulders as if he'd protected her for years.

Once inside, they both shook like puppies, then laughed out loud at the soggy mess they left in the entryway. Rose brushed her sodden hair back from her eyes and frowned when

27

her fingers come away black with soot. 'I keep forgetting how disgusting I must look,' she said, grimacing at Ramsey. 'I'll meet you at the table.' She headed for the ladies room at the back of the restaurant. Ramsey followed the waitress to an empty booth in the opposite direction, but he managed to watch Rose walk the length of the diner.

Her black stockings were snagged and torn and her skirt listed unevenly. Her hair, so dark brown it was almost black, had finally come completely loose from its clip. It hung in long rats' tails down her back, curling to a point just above her waist.

Ramsey slid into the comfortable booth and chuckled to himself as the waitress filled his cup with coffee. He could just imagine Rose's reaction once she got a look at herself in the mirror. Why, if any of his sisters ever got that rumpled, no matter what the circumstances . . . He took a long sip of the strong coffee, grinning at the thought.

Somehow, he had to get Rose DeAngelo talking. Not that he expected her to come right out and tell him she was involved in the hijackings. Life was never that uncomplicated, nor investigations that simply resolved. The original plan had been to head for California with the kind of cargo most often targeted. The big scraper lashed to the trailer behind Ramsey's diesel practically had *Steal me* written all over it. Earth moving equipment was surprisingly easy to resell at a good price on the black market.

With Department of Transportation approval and Handy's cooperation, the sting had been fairly easy to set up. Schedule an attractive shipment, plan a fairly simple route with regular stops and enough deviations from the original plan to look authentic, then file the plan with Acme Insurance. A switch under the dash in the cab of the truck would alert the DOT and Ramsey's partner to any problem, with help only moments away.

Ramsey had no doubt the hijackers would strike. Not only had the thieves stepped up activity in recent weeks, but the thefts were becoming more violent. Ramsey thought of the gun hidden in a secret compartment inside the cab and just as suddenly thought of Rose. He had to avoid violence at all costs, but how?

And how could he maintain contact with Ms. DeAngelo past tonight?

Ramsey was still trying to come up with a plan of action ten minutes and two cups of coffee later when Rose quietly slipped into the booth across the table from him.

He almost choked on the strong brew.

'Are you okay?' she asked, leaning across

29

the Formica table.

Ramsey wondered if this was the same woman, or if somehow there'd been an exchange made in the restroom.

Perfectly applied make-up covered the bruise on her forehead. Hair, dark as mink and twice as shiny, twisted neatly into a tight knot at the nape of her neck. The stink of burnt rubber had been replaced by a clean, soapy fragrance, reminding Ramsey of spring flowers and sunshine. No signs of dirt or soot marred her expensive looking charcoal gray suit.

She looked different, totally professional, distant. Dressed and groomed to perfection, Rose actually appeared intimidating. Ramsey decided he missed the look of vulnerability and in the same thought realized it was better this way.

Against his better judgment, Ramsey tilted his head to one side so that he could see her legs.

Obviously new stockings, tan instead of black, encased Rose's long, slim legs from her black leather pumps to mid thigh. 'Amazing what a lady can find in a simple leather bag, isn't it?' he teased, tearing his gaze away from the sleek perfection of her legs and turning his attention back to her forest green eyes.

She laughed, a deep, throaty chuckle that

tickled his senses, then patted the purse at her side. 'Now you know why I'm so relieved you saved it.' She glanced at her menu. 'Could you order a chef's salad for me? I saw a phone by the restrooms. I need to make a couple of calls.'

'No problem. Anything to drink?'

'Coffee. Black. I'll just be a minute.' Rose scooted back out of the booth, tugging her short skirt as low as she could. She felt the man's searching gaze as she walked to the phone, relieved he couldn't see the broad smile on her face. His startled reaction when she'd returned from the restroom was the nicest compliment she could have received.

Her smile quickly faded when she considered her own reaction to Mike Ramsey. There was an aura of sensuality about the man that stole her breath, an inquiring look in his dark eyes that unnerved her.

Something connected them. Was it the fact he'd saved her life, or did it go beyond that? She couldn't deny the attraction she felt for him. Any more than she could deny wondering what he thought of her.

Briefly she realized James hadn't entered her mind. She was, in fact, more intrigued by Mike Ramsey, a man she didn't know, than by the man she'd been engaged to. It was a sobering thought.

One thing, though. If Mr. Ramsey were at all interested, at least she knew he'd already seen her at her worst. That first look she'd had of herself in the restroom mirror had been quite a shock. Thank goodness she'd been able to repair most of the damage.

A heated blush crept along her neck at the thought of her stringy hair, soot smudged face and rumpled, wet business suit. Definitely not the image she liked to project. James probably would have left her in the car.

But Mike Ramsey hadn't. No, he'd risked his life to save a woman he didn't even know. Even rescued her handbag! Rose wondered how many of her acquaintances would have done the same.

She grabbed her calling card and dialed Denise's home number, still thinking of Ramsey's heroic deed. 'Denise? Hi, it's Rose . . . no, I'm fine, but I had a little accident . . . No, please don't tell James, or Mr. Bonner either. I'm okay . . . What? Fired? Mr. Bonner said I'm fired? Oh . . . ' Well, she'd expected that.

Even so, it put a new spin on things. Rose took a deep breath. This really had been one heck of a day. 'Look, Denise, I can't come back to clean out my desk right now. I'm going to be gone for awhile. I haven't used any vacation time for the past two years and

Acme owes me that much. Just tell Mr. Bonner I had a family emergency . . . No, Denise, I made that up. Everything's fine . . . It's an *excuse*, Denise. If James calls, tell him I needed to get away. I'll explain everything when I get back . . . yes, I really did break our engagement . . . He doesn't think I meant it? He can think what he wants. And if Mr. Bonner was serious and he really did fire me, well . . . I don't quite know what to say. You've been a great secretary. And a good friend . . . everything'll be just fine. I'll call you in a couple of days, okay? G'bye.'

Fired! After all the years she'd spent at Acme, after fighting and clawing her way through office politics and subtle and not so subtle harassment, she'd been fired.

So why didn't it hurt more? She should feel devastated, shouldn't she? Instead, she felt suddenly lighthearted, freer than she'd been in years. At least it made her next decision an easy one.

Rose dialed one more number. She looked at her watch. With the time difference, it should only be six o'clock in California.

The phone rang . . . and kept ringing. Feeling utterly dejected, Rose turned to hang up the phone when she heard a static *click*. The sound of her beloved aunt's voice brought a lump to her throat.

'Aunt Rosa? I'm coming to see you. Is that okay? I want to come home. I need to see the honeysuckle blooming. I need to see you.'

★ ★ ★

Handy's description of Rose DeAngelo as a 'hardhearted, bitchy broad' might not have fit the frightened victim Ramsey'd pulled out of a burning car, but it easily described the sophisticated woman sliding into the vinyl seat across from him.

Tough, professional, sexy as hell. Ramsey knew women like her used their assets. How else could she have climbed the corporate ladder? He'd studied Acme Insurance and he didn't necessarily like the politics he'd read about in the male-dominated company.

Rose DeAngelo not only headed an entire division, she'd reached her position in record time. Picturing her running a hijacking ring didn't require too great a stretch of the imagination.

What about motive? That was easy enough. She wore expensive clothes, hung around with the rich and famous. It cost a lot to maintain a lifestyle to match the Dearborn's, to fit into their niche in society. To be a suitable mate for a wealthy man.

Somehow, Ramsey had to get to know Rose DeAngelo better.

She looked at him and smiled, and once again her image shifted. She had a smile that could light up a room. With her wide mouth and full, glossy lips she looked just like a little girl.

A little girl in a sensational, big girl's body.

He had to quit thinking like this. He should be wondering who she'd called, other than the car rental agency. She'd been gone a long time.

'That salad looks terrific.' She took a bite of the crispy lettuce.

'Did you make your calls?'

'Yeah, but there's no car rental place in town. I can have one delivered from Wheeling, but not until tomorrow.'

'Can you afford the wait? I thought you needed to get back to Pittsburgh.'

'I've changed my plans. I'm going to California.'

'What? That's a long way from Pittsburgh.'

'I know.' Rose sighed. 'I need to visit someone, someone I haven't seen in a long time. The accident today made me realize how important it is that I go now, before it's too late.'

Ramsey took a bite of his sandwich. His thoughts spun. Who could she possibly need to see badly enough that she'd leave her job, her home, her fiancé? 'Almost getting killed'll do that to you,' he said, chewing slowly.

'Yeah.'

'Where in California?' He must be crazy to even consider this. But he still didn't have a plan, and he needed to keep an eye on Ms. DeAngelo. Besides, she was certainly pleasant to look at.

'Jackson. It's a little town in the Mother Lode.'

'I'm headed for Sacramento. I have to deliver the scraper by Saturday.' *If the load isn't hijacked, Ms. DeAngelo.*

'That's only fifty miles from Jackson.'

He could practically read the questions in her dark green eyes. 'I know,' he answered, waiting. The long silence made his palms sweat.

'I don't know you.' She looked away.

'True. But you know my boss. Call Handy. He'll vouch for me.'

'What would Handy say?' Her smile was almost flirtatious.

'That I'm honest, loyal, hardworking, an upstanding citizen.' He smiled back.

'Not to mention brave.' Her expression turned somber, reflective.

'It's nothing. I only did what anyone would have done.'

'It's something to me, Mr. Ramsey. You saved my life.'

'Anytime, Ms. DeAngelo. Now, we were discussing . . . '

'I don't do things like this. Ever.'

'I figured as much. Neither do I.'

'I don't have extra clothes or anything with me.'

'You've got your purse.'

'Thanks to you.'

'Thanks to me.' He swore he could almost hear her think.

'I buy my own meals, split all the expenses?'

'You can even pay for your own room.'

'I can't believe I'd even consider this. I must be crazy.'

Her voice had dropped to a whisper again. It tickled his senses, made him want to touch the line of her jaw, her full lower lip. Made him want her. 'Well, I can't believe I'm asking, so that makes two of us.'

'This has been a really strange day, Mr. Ramsey.'

'Tell me about it, Rose. It's Mike Ramsey, but just Ramsey'll do.' He held his hand out to her, palm up. She grasped his with long, slender fingers. They shook hands. The title of the movie, 'Sleeping With the Enemy,' popped into his head.

'Ramsey it is.' Rose carefully released his hand.

'Finish your dinner, Rose.' Ramsey felt like he was stepping off a cliff, falling into a deep, dark abyss. Tumbling into the secrets hidden behind her forest green eyes. 'We have a load to haul,' he said finally, wondering just how far the road would take them.

3

Tuesday, Illinois

Rose washed her face and tightened her hair into its usual twist, but her thoughts were entirely on the long night of travel, not her bedraggled appearance. She'd awakened this morning with her head cradled in Ramsey's lap. How she'd ended up in that position when they'd started the trip arguing about everything under the sun, she had no idea. The gentle touch of his hand stroking her hair and the solid warmth of his muscular thigh beneath her cheek had soothed her into wakefulness as the truck rolled into the tiny town near Champagne where they planned to rest.

She hadn't even been shocked by the intimacy of his caress. She'd been too busy reveling in the way it felt. Strong, comforting, and oh, so sensual . . .

A sharp rap sounded against the partially open motel door, interrupting her daydreams. Startled, she whirled around.

Ramsey leaned nonchalantly against the frame.

'Hi,' she said, embarrassed when she realized she'd spoken in a breathless whisper. 'I was just . . . ' Her words trailed off as Ramsey stepped through the doorway and into her room.

He filled the space. Rose took a step backward, momentarily ill at ease. Ramsey smiled and the sensation passed.

'All settled in?'

Rose reached for her purse. 'What's there to settle?' She held up her battered leather bag. 'This is all I've got. I need to buy some clothes.'

'That's one good thing about driving all night.' Ramsey held the door for Rose. 'By the time you get where you're going, the stores are open. Want something to eat first?'

'Don't you need to sleep?' Rose locked the door behind them.

'I'll catch some sleep later.'

'If you're sure . . . ' She'd slept for hours while Ramsey drove, but without a clean change of clothes, she'd settled for a quick sponge bath once they'd checked into their rooms. As they crossed the nearly empty parking lot, Rose still felt tattered and exhausted.

Ramsey looked as wonderful as ever, freshly showered, his hair falling damply against the collar of his leather jacket. Even the burn on his face, a brick red slash angling across his right cheekbone from eye to mouth, merely emphasized his good looks.

Somehow it didn't seem quite fair.

He opened the door to the coffee shop. Rose liked the way he guided her to a small booth, his hand a gentle pressure against her back. His manners were impeccable, his speech educated. They'd talked much of the night, at least until she'd fallen asleep. He'd played devil's advocate on every topic their conversation touched, disagreeing to the point of the ridiculous. Her reactions had see-sawed from laughter, to anger, then laughter again. Even now, Rose had absolutely no idea where he really stood on any of the issues they'd fought over, but their conversation had definitely been stimulating.

And completely impersonal. She suddenly realized she didn't know a thing about him, other than the fact he drove a truck for a living. One thing was certain, though. He'd unquestionably forced Rose to reevaluate her opinion of truck drivers.

★   ★   ★

Ramsey couldn't recall ever feeling so aware of a woman before. He fought a steady battle to keep his touch impersonal, to rein in the constant desire to touch her hair, her shoulder, the supple length of her spine. It was a struggle, too, to keep from reevaluating his original opinion of Rose DeAngelo. When he'd talked to Handy this morning, he'd actually defended the woman. Handy's laughter still made his ears burn.

Handy was right, though. Ramsey couldn't trust her. There'd been another hijacking yesterday morning. Handy'd heard it on the evening news and called the company's owner. The victim's agent? Rose DeAngelo. Ramsey didn't accept coincidence, other than the bits and snippets of chance in his own life. Somehow, he had to find the link that tied Rose to the thefts.

'A penny for your thoughts,' Rose said, digging into her plate of scrambled eggs and toast.

Don't you wish. Ramsey stared at the top of her glossy head for a moment, then concentrated on his own breakfast with an occasional glance to watch her eat. *Damn*. She even made eating look sexy. Rose obviously took great pleasure in satisfying her appetite.

Not that it showed on her. Tall and big-boned, she didn't carry an extra ounce of fat. Ramsey found her strong, athletic build, the broad shoulders and self-confident demeanor tremendously appealing. In fact, Ramsey admitted to himself, everything about Rose DeAngelo appealed to him. Like the tip of her tongue, appearing just now at the corner of her lips, catching an errant crumb of toast.

Get your mind back on the job, Ramsey. Remember who you're dealing with. 'I called Handy this morning.' He studied Rose's expression. 'There was another attempted hijacking yesterday. Barton Movers almost lost a shipment of tractor parts to what sounds like the same gang that's pulled the other heists. Happened just south of Cleveland. Something interrupted the theft, but the driver got shot. Handy said his condition's critical.'

'Oh, God,' she whispered. Her face blanched, the fork slipped from between her fingers and clattered to her plate. 'I just talked to Walt Barton last Friday. He's one of my clients. Walt wasn't driving, was he?'

'No, his son. Kid's only twenty-eight years old. Has a wife and three kids. Handy said he'll survive, but it'll be a long recovery.'

'I have to call the office.' With trembling fingers, Rose wiped her lips with her napkin and quickly slipped out of the booth. 'I should never have left. I can't believe this keeps happening.'

'Either you're one hell of an actress or you're innocent,' Ramsey muttered, staring after Rose as she raced to the pay phone at the back of the restaurant. Then a darker thought intruded. *Maybe you just don't like it when your people get sloppy.*

The eggs on Rose's plate had congealed into a cold, greasy mess by the time she returned. Ramsey sipped his coffee, trying to read the emotions clouding Rose's green eyes.

'You want me to order something else?' he asked, gesturing toward her half-eaten meal.

'I can't eat,' Rose said, shuddering. 'I don't even know why I called.' She slid into the booth and pushed her plate away. A waitress appeared and refilled both coffee cups, then took the plate with her.

'I thought you said Barton was one of your clients. Isn't it your job to check on them?'

'I didn't tell you. I got fired yesterday. My secretary told me when I called last night. Not that it matters,' she added bitterly, sipping her coffee.

If she no longer worked for Acme, how would that affect the hijackings? 'What happened? I thought you liked your job,' Ramsey said. *Or is it the moonlighting you prefer?*

'I did.' Rose gazed at the steaming coffee. 'I

was so excited when I got my promotion. I worked hard for it, but the job was interesting, my clients really nice. Then the hijackings started.' Rose turned away and stared out the window. 'I'd been dating James . . . he's my ex-fiancé,' she added, 'for a couple of weeks.'

Ex-fiancé? Ramsey glanced at her left hand, noting the pale band of untanned skin on her ring finger. So, James Dearborn was out of the picture. *Interesting*. Ramsey's gaze settled on Rose's classic profile. Definitely interesting.

'One of my first clients was a friend of his.' Rose turned slowly, raising her chin as she faced Ramsey. Her dark green eyes shimmered, filled with emotion and memories. Ramsey wondered who she saw.

'They'd gone to school together . . . Tim and James. After graduation, Tim worked as a driver for an independent manufacturing company. He hauled specialized equipment parts worth a small fortune. The hijackers stopped him on the one stretch of highway where Tim was most vulnerable. At least no one was badly hurt. That was the first hijacking. Two others occurred within the next eight months. Now, well, they keep happening.'

'I remember reading about the first one.' In

fact, he'd read about all of them in the DOT files, but he wasn't about to explain that to Rose. 'Didn't Acme suspect the driver?'

'My boss wanted to. Luckily, James convinced Mr. Bonner Tim wasn't involved. There weren't any other suspects and the investigation eventually died for lack of evidence.' Rose set her cup back on the table and stared out across the restaurant. Ramsey wasn't certain if her expression was evasive or merely thoughtful.

'I really don't want to talk about it any more,' she said. She shrugged her shoulders and smiled apologetically, then reached for her purse and pulled out enough money to pay her half of the bill.

'I'll get that.' Ramsey grabbed his wallet but Rose stopped him, covering his other hand lightly with hers. Her grasp was friendly, her fingers steady. Her smile now was warm and gracious.

'We have a deal, remember? I buy my own meals and pay for my own room.' Rose's clear green eyes offered no challenge, but Ramsey sensed determination and a steel will.

'You're right,' he said. 'Old habit.'

'It just means your mother trained you right.' Rose gave him a cheeky grin as she slid out of the booth. 'Or did she leave that up to the three sisters you mentioned?'

'Half sisters, actually.' Ramsey followed Rose out of the restaurant. 'They're all younger than I am, so I only had to put up with their hero worship. Of course, their uncompromising adulation was well deserved.'

'I bet.' Rose laughed. 'I just hope they taught you to shop. I learned my skills from my Aunt Rosa, the shopping queen of Amador County.'

'Your aunt? Not your mom?'

'My parents died when I was very young. Aunt Rosa raised me. And that woman can shop.' Rose turned her head and winked back over her shoulder at Ramsey. The impact of that saucy grin and green-eyed wink made his gut clench.

Unwilling to question his reaction, Ramsey followed Rose across the parking lot.

★ ★ ★

The strip mall they walked to had seen better days, but Rose found a feed store filled with everything from blue jeans to baby chicks.

She quickly bought boot cut jeans, a green plaid western-styled shirt with pearl buttons, lots of thick socks and a pair of black leather lace-up roper boots. Ramsey didn't say a word when she handed him the bags and pointed in the direction of a tiny boutique. He did raise his eyebrows while she looked through racks of lacy bras and tiny bikini underpants, but he kept his comments to himself while she made her selections.

Rose added a plain cotton flannel nightgown and a couple of brightly colored turtleneck shirts to the growing pile of clothes, paid the bill with her credit card and handed the bags to Ramsey. Without a word she led him two doors down to a sporting goods store where she quickly found a pair of crosstrainer shoes, a dark green sweatsuit the color of her eyes, a down parka on sale, and a large nylon sports bag. Rose dug through her purse for her wallet, pulled out her credit card one more time and paid the clerk. 'That's it,' she said, signing her name with a flourish.

She tilted her chin to glance up at Ramsey and laughed aloud. Probably thought it was funny that he stood there with his jaw hanging open. He snapped his mouth shut.

'Lady, you're good,' he drawled, glancing at his watch. 'You've just purchased an entire wardrobe in one hour and thirty-two minutes. Must be some kind of record.'

'I warned you . . . Aunt Rosa taught me well.' Rose stuffed her newest purchases into the sports bag.

'I can see that. C'mon. Let's get back to the motel and catch a few hours sleep. Then, I want to see you in some of those new clothes.'

'You won't recognize me in my new Wrangler jeans,' Rose said, leading him out of the store.

'That's not the outfit I was thinking of,' Ramsey muttered, imagining, instead, the lacy ivory colored bra and panties she'd purchased. *Dream on, Ramsey.* Silently laughing at himself, he juggled the slippery plastic bags filled with his share of Rose's new wardrobe and followed her to the street corner across from the motel.

A sudden commotion caught Ramsey's attention. He turned just as a scraggly teenaged boy on rollerblades whizzed by, grabbing the strap of Rose's handbag as he passed.

'Let go!' Rose shouted, hanging onto her purse and swinging at the thief in a wide arc. Ramsey dropped the shopping bags and captured the slightly built boy by the waist, lifting him completely off the ground. The boy's feet, encased in heavy rollerblades, flailed against Ramsey's legs.

'Oomph!' Ramsey dropped the purse-snatcher and clutched his shins. The youngster struggled to his feet, his rollerblades sliding this way and that.

'Don't let him get away.' Rose glared at Ramsey. He glared back. Spinning around, she raced after the boy, tackled him and straddled his legs, holding his feet to the ground. Her gray skirt split along one side from hem to waist and her new stockings shredded at the knees, but she didn't let go of her prisoner. 'Aren't you going to help me?' she demanded, hanging onto the boy's bony legs.

Ramsey doubled over, laughing. Rose might sound indignant as hell, but she looked absolutely gorgeous. Cheeks flushed, green eyes flashing, long hair once again all undone and tangling to her waist. Only this time, instead of barely escaping a burning car, she'd out-mugged a mugger.

'You've definitely got your own technique, lady,' Ramsey gasped, clasping the winded boy's skinny arm at the same time as he grabbed Rose's outstretched hand. He helped both of them to their feet, steadying the boy when his rollerblades threatened to slip out from under him.

'Now, do you want to apologize to the lady before or after I call the police?'

The boy's eyes grew wide in fear, then just as suddenly narrowed. His expression turned sullen.

'How old are you?' Ramsey tightened his grip.

'Sixteen.'

'I'd say more like ten, wouldn't you, Rose?'

'I'm not ten, I'm twelve.' Glowering, the boy looked away.

'What do ya think we should do with him, Rose?'

She tried to read Ramsey's expression. It was obvious he didn't really want to involve the police.

Tires screeched. A new luxury sedan slid to a halt just beyond the corner, then backed up. A large, nicely dressed man jumped out of the car and ran around the back to confront Ramsey.

'Let go of my son,' he demanded, reaching for the boy.

'Not so fast.' Ramsey maintained his grip. 'This young man tried to steal the lady's purse. We were debating whether or not to call the police.'

'I did not,' the boy shouted, struggling against Ramsey.

Rose looked at the father and saw defeat in the man's tired, gray eyes. 'It's true,' she said, feeling the father's anquish.

'Don't lie to me, Jess. Not anymore.' The man reached for his son. 'The school called . . . he cut class again. He's started hanging out down here at the mall, and . . . I'm terribly sorry. I don't know what to say.' He shrugged helplessly. 'Since his mother left, I . . . ' His voice trailed off, and his shoulders slumped in helpless frustration.

'Dad? What's wrong, Dad?'

'Everything, Jess.' The man clenched the boy's thin shoulders in both hands, forcing his son to look at him. 'Don't you understand what you've done? You tried to steal this woman's purse. She might call the police . . . maybe she should.' He reached in his pocket for a handkerchief and blew his nose. 'Jess, I don't want my only son to end up in jail.'

'It was a joke, Dad.' The boy's face crumbled. He turned to Rose, his expression remorseful. 'I'm sorry. The guys dared me. I didn't think.'

'Maybe next time you will.' Ramsey leaned over and picked up the spilled packages. He turned to the boy's father. 'We're not going to press charges, but maybe you ought to check on the kids your son hangs out with.'

'I intend to. Thank you, thank you both. C'mon, Jess. We have some talking to do.' He opened the car door on the passenger side. Jess slid into the seat, looking small and contrite as his father closed the door.

'Thanks,' the older man whispered to Rose and Ramsey, his voice choked with emotion. Rose watched him get into the car, saw him pull his son close and hug the boy before the sedan eased away from the curb.

'I know you think I should have called the police. He committed a crime, but . . . '

'But I'll bet you had your reasons,' Rose said, noticing the tear in her skirt for the first time. 'Maybe you'll tell me about them after we've both had some sleep.'

Ramsey yawned, then leaned over and rubbed his shins. 'If he stays out of jail, that kid's got a future in soccer. And you, my dear, would make one helluva tackle.'

Rose flashed Ramsey the most disgusted look she could muster, then hitched her purse over her shoulder and grabbed the sports bag full of new clothes. She didn't look to see if he was following with the rest of her bags when she crossed the street and headed back to the motel.

It was barely Tuesday and she'd already had the most harrowing week of her life.

★   ★   ★

Rose checked her watch, then quickly rolled and stuffed her new clothes into the sports bag. Ramsey should be here any moment. She dressed in the green plaid western shirt, blue jeans and black boots, then wadded up all the tags and threw them in the trash. Right on top of her ruined business suit.

The expensive charcoal gray skirt and jacket had gone into the trash the moment Rose took them off. They'd cost almost a week's wages when she'd first gone to work for Acme Insurance. The designer suit had made her feel successful, professional. She'd felt self-confident and strong when she wore it, a woman ready to tackle the world.

It certainly felt good to throw it away.

'That must mean something,' Rose muttered, unsure, however, exactly what. She pulled her hair up into its usual twist and reached for the clip to hold it against the nape of her neck, then paused.

The woman looking back at her out of the foggy motel mirror wasn't a complete stranger, but she definitely had a sparkle in her eyes that had been missing for far too long.

Almost defiantly, Rose loosened the heavy twist of hair and let it fall, long and slightly waving, almost to her waist. She plucked a single gray hair from just above her right temple, then stuck her tongue out at the image in the mirror.

'You about ready in there?' Ramsey asked, following his question with a quick rap against the door.

Rose felt her skin flush, thankful the door

was shut and Ramsey hadn't caught her making faces in the mirror. 'Yeah,' she said, crossing the small room and opening the door. 'C'mon in.'

The spicy scent of Chinese food wafted ahead of Ramsey as he entered her room, his arms filled with paper bags and cardboard cartons.

'I sure hope you like Mandarin,' he said, carrying the packages to the small round table next to Rose's unmade bed. 'The guy at the front desk said the take-out from this place is a lot better than the diner here at the motel.'

'Do you think you bought enough?' Rose asked sarcastically, eyeing the wide array of foods Ramsey was arranging on the tiny table. Cartons of shrimp, fried rice, chow mein and a variety of vegetable dishes covered the surface, enough for at least a half-dozen large appetites.

'We can always get more, Ms. Piggy.' He handed Rose a paper plate and set of wooden chopsticks, then pulled the vinyl covered chair back from the table so she could sit down.

Rose sat with her back to the bed, facing Ramsey across the small table. Their knees bumped. When she moved her legs to avoid his, they bumped again. 'Excuse me,' Rose muttered, at the same time Ramsey said, 'Sorry.'

'Small table,' he said, not meeting Rose's eyes. She grinned, recognizing the sudden restraint between the two of them for what it was, an awareness that had merely been lurking in the background since they'd met. Still smiling, Rose served herself small portions from the steaming cartons.

'Tastes good.' Rose took another bite of shrimp. She looked up from her plate, expecting to catch Ramsey's gaze. He was looking beyond her, his eyes dark gray pools beneath heavy lashes. Staring at her unmade bed. A heated flush spread across Rose's chest and up her throat. She licked her lips, watching Ramsey, wondering at the thoughts behind those dark, dark eyes.

★　★　★

Rose's bed had a freshly rumpled look, the pillow still carried the indention of her head. The sheets might hold the warmth from her body even now. Ramsey swallowed, forcing his thoughts out of the realm of fantasy they'd so easily entered.

This woman was still his chief suspect; if not in charge of, at the very least an accomplice in a string of violent hijackings. It wasn't difficult to believe when she wore her dark business suit with her hair pulled into a tight roll at the nape of her neck. Dressed professionally, she looked capable of achieving anything she wanted, legal or otherwise.

But Ramsey hadn't expected the visceral reaction, the physical rush he'd felt when he saw Rose in a pair of tight blue jeans and her green plaid shirt. The green matched her eyes, an improbable color like springtime fields after a long, wet winter. And her hair. He'd only seen it mussed and stringy, or slicked against her head, twisted and clipped in place. Now her hair hung long and loose, falling across one eye and hanging in shimmering waves over her shoulders. Tiny wisps framed her face, a sable halo of curls that softened her finely cut features.

If Rose DeAngelo had been a threat to Ramsey before, she was even more dangerous like this. Soft and inviting, her lips slightly parted and shiny from the oil of the fried shrimp she'd just tasted. As if reading his thoughts, Rose slowly licked her upper lip, then dabbed at her mouth with her paper napkin.

'The clerk was right, this is really good,' she said, not meeting Ramsey's gaze.

'Wonderful,' Ramsey answered, unable to take his eyes off the glossy fullness of her lips.

The table seemed to shrink between them until Ramsey saw nothing but the subtle question in Rose's eyes and the rumpled, unmade bed behind her. He reached out, touching the silky strands of hair framing her face. She rewarded him with the slight pressure of her cheek as she leaned into his hand.

One kiss. That's all, just one, he thought, turning his head to match his lips to hers, thrilled by her obvious acceptance of the inevitable. And it was inevitable, a kiss to signify either a beginning or an ending.

Giving into the need to increase the pressure of his mouth on hers, to draw her soft moan of pleasure into his own lungs, to taste her more completely, Ramsey shifted slightly in his chair.

And knocked the half-empty carton of chicken chow mein right into Rose's lap.

★　★　★

'I can't believe I did that,' Ramsey said, still chuckling as he handed Rose a towel he'd dampened in the bathroom sink.

What? Kiss me, or dump dinner in my lap? Rose avoided meeting his eyes as she wiped at the slimy mess staining her new jeans. What had she been thinking, to kiss him back like that? What had he been thinking, to kiss her?

'Don't worry about it,' she said, recalling the firm pressure of his lips on hers, the taste of him, the callused tenderness of his fingertips along her cheek.

Just thinking about their kiss made her heart-rate soar. She wondered what would have happened if they hadn't been quite so clumsy. She wondered if he'd kiss her again.

'Did you get enough?' he asked, picking up the scattered remnants of their dinner.

'Excuse me?' Rose's head shot up at his question.

'Dinner. Did you have enough dinner? I thought I'd stick the rest of this in the ice chest so we can get moving.'

'Oh, yeah, thanks. I had plenty.' Mortified, she felt the hot flush spread once again across her collarbones. She had to quit thinking about that kiss. Obviously Ramsey didn't intend to mention it. He probably regretted kissing her as much as she regretted that he'd stopped. And Lord, how she hated to admit, she hadn't wanted him to stop.

★　★　★

Rose adjusted her seat belt so she could curl up on the broad bench seat inside the big diesel. She felt warm and comfortable in her sweatsuit. The freshly rinsed jeans hung drying on a hook just behind the seat.

Ramsey hadn't said much since they'd left the motel but the traffic had been heavy and Rose didn't want to distract him. Now, though, they were practically alone on the broad interstate. Her thoughts returned to the incident earlier in the day, carefully avoiding any speculation over Ramsey's kiss. She couldn't possibly dissect her feelings with him sitting so close beside her, but maybe she could find out more about him. It couldn't hurt to ask.

'Are you gonna tell me why you didn't want to have that little thief arrested?' she finally asked. 'If his father hadn't come along, would you have just let him go?'

'Probably,' Ramsey said after a long pause. Then he grinned. 'But I would have put the fear of God into him first.'

'And how would you go about doing that?' Rose asked, surprised when his smiling lips thinned into a firm, straight line.

'I guess by telling him what getting arrested is like. It's not a particularly good experience, especially when you're only twelve.'

'You say that with the voice of authority.' Ramsey couldn't actually know what it was like . . . could he?

'Exactly.' He glanced in Rose's direction,

his expression somber.

'You were arrested? When you were just a little boy?' The haunted look in Ramsey's eyes told Rose much more, she was certain, than he wanted her to know. She tried to imagine him as a child, so troubled he'd ended up breaking the law. 'Do you want to talk about it?'

'There's not much to talk about. Besides, it's a long story.'

'We've got all night.'

'And a lot of ground to cover.' Ramsey checked the rearview mirror. 'Another time, maybe.'

'Okay.' Rose grabbed a map off the dashboard and tried to ignore the uneasy silence that settled over the cab. Spreading the map out across the dash, she recalled the route Handy Hannibal had described.

South, she thought, *through Denver and on into southern California, then north to Sacramento*. The longer route avoided the risk of bad weather and should keep them well out of the early spring storm track.

So why was Ramsey driving north? 'I thought you were going to take Highway 70,' she said, folding the map up and slipping it into the compartment on the door.

'I would have cut across at Indianapolis if I was gonna take 70. Besides, I never said which way I was planning to go.' Ramsey checked his rearview mirror. 'Only that I was delivering this shipment to Sacramento and you to Jackson. It's a lot shorter to take Interstate 80 through Reno. That'll drop us directly into Sacramento.'

'Did you remember to file your route changes with Acme?' Rose asked. She knew it hadn't been done before she left the office Monday morning.

'It's taken care of.' Ramsey turned his attention back to the rain-slick road. He glanced at Rose sitting across the cab from him, all curled up on the wide bench seat. Right now, she was the only one, other than his partner Kathleen, who knew of his change in plans. He wasn't even going to tell Handy his truck was currently heading along Interstate 80 instead of 70, as they'd planned.

He wasn't going to tell anyone but Rose. And as much as he wanted to relive the moment, he was going to do his damnedest not to think about the kiss they'd shared, not to remember the gentle pressure of her lips against his, or her sweet taste. No, he planned to give Rose DeAngelo just enough rope to hang herself, then hope like hell his hunch was wrong.

Because if the hijackers struck between here and Sacramento, it could only mean Rose DeAngelo had set him up.

4

Wednesday, Nebraska

'Wake up, sleepyhead. Open those bright green eyes. We'll stay here until the storm blows over.'

'Storm? What storm?' Rose blinked awake, stiff and groggy after sleeping curled up in the front seat. Vaguely she recalled Ramsey tucking a blanket around her shoulders as they'd crossed the Iowa state line late Tuesday evening.

'The storm that's closed the highway for the rest of the night.' Ramsey peered at Rose through damp, spiky eyelashes. Snow dusted the shoulders of his leather jacket. 'We'll have to share a cabin,' he said, 'but it's got two beds. It's the best I could do at this hour.'

'What time is it?' Rose sat up and shoved her tangled hair out of her eyes. The snow swirled against the windshield, multicolored confetti in the garish reflection of the motel's palm tree-shaped neon sign. 'Desert Palm Hideaway' blinked incongruously, flickering pink and green through the silent storm.

'Almost four. You were sleeping so soundly

I just drove on through. We're in Nebraska, near Omaha. You missed Iowa altogether.' He grinned and stepped back, from the truck. 'C'mon. This place really is a dump, but it has little cabins with woodstoves, so if the power goes out we won't freeze.'

'I can't believe I slept through a whole state,' Rose mumbled, wrapping the heavy wool blanket around her shoulders. Trailing it behind her, she followed Ramsey through the wet snow, into the last of a group of small cabins ringing the parking lot. 'Oh my.' She paused, hand over her mouth, in the doorway. 'This'll wake me up.'

It took a conscious effort to shut her mouth as she stared about the garishly decorated room. 'Now I know how Genie must have felt, living in that brass lamp.'

'At least it's clean.' Ramsey chuckled, a pleasant rumble emanating from deep within his chest. 'Beats sleeping in the cab of the truck.'

'I don't know,' Rose said, brushing lightly past him. 'I was doing fairly well in there up 'til a few minutes ago.' She yawned and stretched and the blanket slipped off her shoulders. Ramsey grabbed it before it could fall to the floor and without a word carefully wrapped it back around her shoulders. 'Thank you.' Rose clasped it tightly against her chest and shivered.

'I'll have it warm in here in a minute.' Ramsey added kindling to the freestanding woodstove in one corner of the gaudy little room and lit the fire. The air began to warm up almost immediately. He watched the flames for a moment, then grinned at Rose. 'You're awfully quiet for a change.'

'I'm not going to say another word.'

'Only because the decor leaves you speechless, right?' Ramsey straightened and brushed his hands against his thighs. 'I'll get our bags and the ice chest. I doubt there's anything open at this hour, but the leftover Chinese food sounds pretty good.'

'At four in the morning? Yuck.' Rose stuck her tongue out and made a face. The deep rumble of Ramsey's laughter followed him out into the storm, leaving the room in lonely silence when he shut the door. Rose took a quick look around her, giggling at the faded, red velvet curtains draped over each bed, the green and black striped wallpaper and the abundance of fake brass.

'Desert chic for the desert sheik,' she quipped as she headed into the bathroom to splash cold water on her face. The decorations in the bathroom were even gaudier than the rest of the cabin. She closed her eyes against the glare from the overhead lights reflected off embossed, gold foil wallpaper. Driving at night already had her internal clock totally confused. Ramsey's choice of motel threatened to short circuit any surviving brain cells.

Rose slowly opened her eyes and stared at her puffy, sleep-swollen face in the gilt-edged mirror, doing her best to ignore the bug-eyed portrait of a turbaned sultan glaring at her from the wall behind the toilet. If Ramsey hadn't already seen her at her worst right after the wreck, Rose figured she'd be really upset to let him see her like this. Silently she contemplated the character of a man who didn't seem to be hung up on the perfect hairstyle or immaculate make-up.

The cabin shook and Rose jumped, her heart thumping erratically. Someone pounded on the door. Suddenly wide awake, she raced out of the bathroom.

'Rose! Rose, open up. Hurry.'

'What's the matter?' She jerked the door open.

Pelted with blowing snow, Ramsey practically blew into the cabin. In his arms he carried what first appeared to be a bundle of damp and tattered rags. Carefully, he set his burden down on the closest bed, then pulled a heavy shawl back to reveal the face of a young, dark haired girl. Her eyes were closed.

'She must've crawled into the cab to get out of the storm. She's freezing, poor thing. Get her out of these wet clothes while I call 911.'

'Okay.' Rose carefully slipped the heavy jacket from around the girl's shoulders. Her tiny body shivered uncontrollably. 'She can't be more than twelve or thirteen,' Rose whispered. 'What would she be doing out in this kind of weather?'

The child's eyes fluttered open, wide and frightened. Rose smiled reassuringly and helped her sit up. 'What's your name, sweetie?' she asked, hoping her voice would calm the girl. 'You must be so cold . . . I'm just going to help you out of these wet things and wrap you up in some warm blankets.'

The child moaned painfully. Ramsey set the phone quietly back in its cradle. 'I've got bad news, Rose,' he said. 'The phone's out.'

'I've got worse news.' Stunned, Rose tried to project a sense of calm she didn't feel. She turned to Ramsey, locking his gray eyed gaze with her own. 'This little girl's pregnant and I think she's in labor.'

'What?' he hissed. 'She's too little to be . . . '

'I'm almost nineteen. I'm not a little girl,' the young woman gasped, dark eyes flashing. She took a deep breath, obviously searching for control. After a few more panting breaths, she let out a huge sigh of relief. 'Please, can you help me? I need to go to my aunt's. My name is Mary Lawson. My Aunt Vicky lives in Lincoln. If you can just take me there . . . '

'Mary, we're not going anywhere.' Ramsey knelt beside the bed and covered the girl's icy hands with both of his. She was so small, so cold. Her dark hair fell long and straight, surprisingly clean, considering her ragged clothes and what he guessed to be her homeless state. He felt awkward and helpless, and glanced at Rose for support. She shrugged, the gesture totally unreassuring.

He squeezed the girl's cold hands, offering what little comfort he could. There wasn't much. 'The storm's turned into a full-blown blizzard.' He spoke softly, reassuring her as much as he could. 'Roads are closed. We can't get out, but I don't want you to worry. My name's Mike Ramsey and this is Rose. We'll help you, I promise. Right now, I'm going to the manager's office, see if she's got any ideas. You'll be just fine.' *I hope*, he amended, looking desperately at Rose. 'You're sure she's in labor?'

'Yes.' Both women answered as Mary doubled over, clutching her middle. Rose wrapped her arms around the girl's thin shoulders and looked helplessly at Ramsey.

'I'll be right back.' Ramsey glanced from one face to the other, then lunged for the door. He disappeared in a blast of frigid wind and swirling snow, slamming the door behind him as he made his escape. The sound of the girl's labored breathing filled the room. When her contraction ended, the silence was absolute.

Rose looked at Mary, suddenly disconcerted when the girl giggled and gestured toward the door with a nod of her head. 'Man, he was sure in some hurry to get outta here.'

'You got that impression, too, hmm?' Rose smiled warmly at Mary, inviting her confidence. 'He'll be back. Now, are you going to tell me what's going on?' she asked, keeping her tone casual.

'You mean besides me having a baby in your motel room? And lady, this is one ugly room.' Mary's voice had a cocky edge to it, a streetwise slant that reminded Rose of the little thief on rollerblades. But at least Jess had a father who cared about him. Mary looked as if she had no one.

'You said you were trying to get to Lincoln.' Rose took Mary's hand in hers and was surprised when the girl didn't try to pull away, but instead returned her grasp.

'My aunt lives there. She doesn't know

about . . . ' Mary gestured toward her swollen middle with her free hand, 'but she'll let me stay with her. I think.' Her voice cracked. Rose felt the tears well up in her own eyes.

'What about your baby's father?' Rose was certain Mary's hand turned to ice in hers.

'No.'

'Mary, there are laws that make the father at least financially responsible for . . . '

'I said *no*.' Her hand tightened in Rose's and she gasped as another contraction hit.

'Oh, Mary.' Rose pulled the sobbing girl into her arms. After the contraction subsided, she held Mary close, listening with horror to the child's story, crying with her, as much for Mary and her unborn child as for the dreams the girl had been denied.

After awhile, Mary pulled away from Rose. She sat huddled on the edge of the bed while Rose went into the bathroom for a damp washcloth. By the time she'd returned, Mary's spine had straightened and the girl flashed her a cocky grin. 'I'm gonna be okay, ya know.' She took the washcloth Rose handed to her and wiped her face, her motions defiant.

'I think you are.' Rose smiled, fighting the urge to pull Mary into her arms again and comfort her like the child she hadn't been allowed to be. So young to be so tough.

Thoughts of her Aunt Rosa leapt to mind, of the love Rose had received when her parents died, the almost seamless transition from one caring home to another. Without the steadfast nurturing from Aunt Rosa, might she have ended up as alone and troubled as this young woman?

Thank you, Aunt Rosa. 'And thank you, Ramsey,' she whispered. *Thanks for taking me home.*

★ ★ ★

Almost an hour later, Rose glanced up at the sound of a key turning in the lock. The force of the storm shook the small cabin when Ramsey opened the door. His hair and eyebrows looked frosted, his leather coat stiff and frozen. At Rose's silent entreaty, he shook his head.

'The night manager's no help. I think she got into the medicinal brandy. I tried the cell phone, but that's out, too, so I hiked a ways down the road to another pay phone. I think the whole system must be out. I grabbed the lantern in case the power goes, but I couldn't find your bag in the truck. Did you already bring it in?' He looked around the room. 'Where's the girl?'

'She's in the shower.' Rose nodded in the

direction of the small bathroom. 'Her contractions have slowed down some and I figured she'd be more comfortable in my flannel nightgown.'

'Did you find out anything about her?' Ramsey checked the woodstove and added another piece of oak from the filled wood box.

'Her father kicked her out and she's been staying with friends. Her mother's dead. She's trying to get to her aunt's house. The baby's not due for two weeks.'

'Good Lord! She's just a baby, herself.' Ramsey sat on the edge of the second double bed, opposite Rose.

'She comes across like she's so tough, but down inside she's scared to death. It's really awful,' Rose added, glancing toward the bathroom. The sound of running water continued. 'She'd just been awarded a college scholarship and went out with a girlfriend to celebrate. A bunch of boys grabbed them and assaulted both girls. When her father found out she'd gotten pregnant, he kicked her out of the house.'

'Even though it wasn't her fault?'

'She said her father didn't see it like that. He said she asked for trouble by going out at night. In their neighborhood . . . '

'I could never disown my own child.'

'I know.' The moment stretched between them. What was it about this man that affected her so? Finally, Rose blinked and turned away. 'Well,' she said, 'Mary's got an amazing attitude. She's a survivor and she's still an optimist, even after what's happened. The utter resiliency of the young, I guess.'

She grinned when Mary's voice, muffled by the sound of the shower, drifted through the room. It only took a moment to recognize the words to a popular Whitney Houston song. 'See what I mean?'

Ramsey just shook his head.

'Ever deliver a baby, Ramsey?' Rose almost laughed aloud at the stricken look on his face.

'That's not in my repertoire. How about you?'

'Calves and lambs,' Rose answered. 'I don't think it's quite the same, although my aunt used to say delivering babies is just like lambs, but without the fuzz.'

Ramsey cocked his head to one side, studying her. 'So, you're a farm girl? You don't look the type.'

'Right down to my 4-H uniform.' Rose grinned and Ramsey felt a sudden surge of anger. He wanted to kiss her, not suspect her of theft. 'Unfortunately,' she added, looking sadly toward the bathroom door, 'pulling calves doesn't prepare you for delivering people babies.'

'I don't think we have to worry,' Ramsey said, with more confidence than he felt. 'First babies don't come all that fast. The storm'll probably be over by the time she's ready to deliver.'

'Rose? Rose, are you out there?'

The anxious call from the bathroom startled both of them.

'Having another contraction, sweetie?' *Calm*, Rose thought. She had to sound calm . . . but how, when panic felt so natural?

'I'll be okay. Just a minute.'

It was at least ten minutes longer before Mary opened the bathroom door. Rose and Ramsey had almost reached the point of forcing the door open, but suddenly Mary was standing there in the open doorway surrounded by warm clouds of billowing steam.

Rose's cotton gown hung to the floor on the tiny girl, but her protruding belly left no doubt as to her condition. Rose was relieved to see Mary's cocky grin back in place. The girl bent over and wrapped a fluffy white towel around her dark hair.

'Don't worry. I'm okay. I was just surprised. I think my water broke in the shower. Thank goodness it happened there!

What a mess. Oh, hi, Mr. Ramsey.' She looked up as if nothing momentous were happening and tucked the towel firmly in place. 'Doesn't that mean the baby's coming?'

'Yes, it does, doesn't it, oh, authority-on-first-babies.' Rose glanced sideways at Ramsey. 'The expert, here, was just informing me how first babies usually take a long time arriving.'

'This one's already two weeks early. I think he's in a hurry. I'm really sorry to put you out like this, I mean, you don't even know me and here I am wearing your nightgown and having a baby in your room.' Mary's impudent demeanor began to slip, but then she grinned at Ramsey. 'I take it you couldn't find the local midwife.'

Only a teenager could find humor in this situation. Rose prayed Mary wouldn't realize how frightened she and Ramsey really were.

'The local midwife's unavailable,' Ramsey answered, 'but you've got Rose, deliverer of baby lambs, and Mike Ramsey . . . '

'Water boiler extraordinaire,' Rose added. 'And as far as not knowing each other, I'm sure we'll get past that before the baby's here.'

Mary's already fair complexion suddenly turned chalky. 'Oh . . . ' she whispered, as if the reality of her situation were finally sinking in. Rose sent a silent prayer heavenward for the girl. To be so young and so alone.

'You'll be fine.' Rose glanced at Ramsey who stared solemnly at Mary's middle. Reality must have slammed into the truck driver as well. 'Everything will be just fine,' she repeated, with more conviction than she felt. *Let's just hope Ramsey survives.*

Suddenly, Mary groaned and doubled over. Ramsey moved out of the way and Rose helped the girl to the closest bed.

'C'mon, now. We talked about breathing. In, out, remember?'

Ramsey checked his watch and waited until the contraction was over. 'Is there anything I should I do?' he asked when Mary's breathing returned to normal. He groaned dramatically when together Rose and Mary ordered, 'Boil water.'

'Why did I know you were going to say that?'

Rose looked down at Mary and the girl giggled. 'How can you laugh at a time like this?' Rose whispered, more to herself than to the child.

Mary gazed up at Rose with the eyes of an old soul. Where Rose expected desperation, she saw fierce determination, a strength far beyond the young woman's years. 'What choice do I have?' Mary asked. Her words ended on a gasp of pain as another contraction hit.

Rose grasped Mary's hand and prayed.

★ ★ ★

The storm broke around noon Wednesday. Neither Ramsey nor Rose noticed when the roaring wind stilled. Ramsey was too busy kneeling behind Mary, supporting her narrow shoulders and wiping sweat away from her eyes and Rose was totally involved in helping to bring Victoria Rose Lawson into the world.

An hour later, as mother and newborn slept behind the garish velvet drape, Rose curled up next to Ramsey on the extra bed. The sense of exhilaration hadn't left her, the feeling she had taken part in an event that would leave her forever changed.

She snuggled against Ramsey's shoulder, feeling the warmth of him along her entire length. His even breathing told her he slept, finally, after the long night of driving and the hours spent with Mary. The roads might still be closed and the phone dead, but a sense of peace and hope filled the room.

Soon they would have to take Mary to a hospital and move on, soon they would arrive in California and Ramsey would go his way while Rose went hers. But not just yet. Now, she absorbed his heat and felt as if she'd known him forever, would be beside him, forever.

How could so much change in three short days?

Has it only been three days? Impossible. Smiling, dreaming the sweet smell of honeysuckle, Rose drifted off to sleep.

★   ★   ★

The emergency clinic where they took Mary and the baby later that evening after the roads were cleared was only a few blocks away. Mary's Aunt Vicky arrived shortly before dawn and all of Rose's fears for the young woman and her daughter evaporated in the warmth of Vicky's hug and the compassion in her smile.

Mary and Victoria Rose were going home. Once again, Rose thought of Aunt Rosa.

They exchanged hugs and tears and addresses and parted with a sense of family that still filled Rose when she and Ramsey arrived back at the Desert Palms Hideaway.

'Should I pack?' Rose stretched and yawned, then stared blankly at her belongings piled near the sports bag in the corner. The thought of climbing into the truck for a long night of travel had no appeal whatsoever.

'Nope.' Ramsey grabbed her shoulders and steered her toward the freshly made bed against the wall. 'I'm going to get us something to eat and then we're both going to get some sleep. As emotionally and physically drained as I am right now, I don't think my insurance agent would like to see me behind the wheel.'

'Your ex-insurance agent admires your sensibility.' Rose attempted a smile, but it took too much effort. Instead, she plopped down on the bed. 'I'll wait right here,' she said, stretching out on the surprisingly comfortable bed, then snuggling into the thick quilt. Her semi-conscious mind barely registered the quiet click of the lock as Ramsey left the room.

⋆   ⋆   ⋆

Ramsey opened the door and set the bags of fried chicken, potato salad and soft drinks on the table. Rose slept on, her hands tucked beneath her cheek, her lips slightly parted, a quizzical frown wrinkling her brow. He wondered what she dreamed, what thoughts flitted through her sleeping mind.

She smiled in her sleep, arched her back, then shifted her legs, drawing one up near her chest. His mouth went dry and he wondered if she dreamed of him.

Damn. This was not good. She was a suspect, the *main* suspect. He shouldn't have to keep reminding himself.

At least he'd been able to talk to his DOT partner. Just in time, too, he mused, since he'd been out of contact for over twenty-four hours. Kathleen Malone was a good agent, but she tended to be impatient. He didn't want her jumping the gun and putting an all-points bulletin out on the rig. She'd promised to let Handy know everything was okay without divulging any more information than she had to. Ramsey knew he could trust her to be discreet.

Thank goodness she hadn't questioned his reasons for traveling with Rose, or the change in route. Kathleen trusted his decisions. Ramsey only wished he had as much faith in himself as his partner did.

Hell, he'd hardly even thought about the job, or the hijackings, or the reason he was making this fool delivery in the first place, not since he'd met Rose. It was becoming more and more difficult to remember he was running an investigation into a multi-million dollar theft ring and that the woman who would be sharing his room tonight was his chief suspect.

That's gonna be fun to explain in my

report, he thought, dreading Kathleen's reaction. She could come up with a wise-ass comment even when he wasn't doing something stupid. She'd have a field day with this one.

Rose stretched, then rubbed her eyes. Ramsey imagined leaning over and kissing her into wakefulness, drawing her into his arms and tasting those full lips that parted now so invitingly.

Just as quickly he forced the image out of his mind, replacing it with his memory of the incriminating DOT files on Rose. He certainly never thought he'd have to worry about falling in love with a suspect. This was definitely new territory and it wasn't worth the risk.

Rose jerked awake as Ramsey noisily dug through the bags and arranged their meal on the desk. 'I didn't hear you come in,' she said, yawning. 'That smells good. Chicken?'

He merely nodded his reply.

The meal was a quiet affair. Ramsey was unusually somber, but he'd barely slept at all since yesterday. Bedtime was a relief, even though they shared the same room. Rose had been able to put the kiss out of her mind with all the events of the past few hours and she refused to dwell on it tonight. Physically and mentally she felt as tapped out as she knew

Ramsey must be. He fell into a deep sleep almost as soon as his head hit the pillow.

Still wearing the warm green sweatsuit, Rose crawled into her own bed. In the reflected light from the flashing motel sign, she took a moment to study the man sleeping only inches away from her. The sight of him, the sculpted planes of his lean torso, the masculine perfection of his broad shoulders and powerful looking arms, caught her gaze and held it.

She thought of him helping Mary during the birth, his calm words of encouragement to both Mary and herself. Then he'd cradled Victoria Rose against him. The tender image brought tears to Rose's eyes . . . again. For such a powerfully built man he was wonderfully gentle with the fragile bundle in his arms. To be held against that chest, swept up in those arms . . . Rose's eyes drifted shut on the sweet fantasy, secure in the fact he slept so close.

She hardly knew him. Still, she felt a link with Ramsey, a knowledge of having shared an intimate event with a stranger, a sense they were strangers no more.

5

Thursday, late afternoon, Nebraska

Rose stuffed the last of her things into the sports bag and took a final look at the tiny cabin she and Ramsey had shared. When she'd first walked into the gaudy little room with its velvet paintings and garish decor, she'd never imagined she would be forever changed even before it was time to leave. Now, she looked about with a bittersweet sense of fondness, a heart filled with memories of sharing the intimacy of a baby's birth with Ramsey.

Ramsey. The graphic image of broad shoulders, strong hands and fathomless gray eyes filled her mind. Would she ever get over the sweet taste of his lips, the look of wonder on his face when he'd kissed her?

Or the way he looked holding the baby? Those brawny arms cradling Victoria, his tender smile as he whispered to her, the dark curve of his eyelashes and the crinkles at the corners of his eyes when he gazed at the precious bundle in his arms.

His look of regret had been genuine when

he'd handed Victoria over to her mother, then driven away from the hospital. What had his thoughts been? Had he imagined his own child, his future?

Rose visualized that same gentleness, that intense concentration directed at her. She'd never once realized how sexy a strong man holding a tiny baby could be. Had never considered the effect it would have on her.

Ramsey opened the door. Startled out of her fantasies, Rose turned.

'C'mon, Rose. The trailer's hooked up, the truck's got fuel, and we're way behind schedule. Did you get in touch with your aunt?

'Yeah.' Rose grabbed her bag and gave the room one final glance. 'I left her a message so she wouldn't worry.'

Ramsey grunted his reply. She noticed his brief pause just before he shut the door, a moment when he looked beyond her, into the little cabin. She wondered what memories Mike Ramsey would take with him of their stay in this room.

Moments later, load secured and bag stowed, Ramsey eased the big truck out onto the freeway. Rose settled into her corner and watched him as he checked the rearview mirror, then skillfully merged with the flow of traffic.

They traveled in silence while the sky darkened around them.

'Do you think Mary and the baby will be okay?' Rose spoke so softly, she wondered if Ramsey even heard her over the roar of the diesel.

After a long pause, he finally spoke. 'Her Aunt Vicky seems like a pretty terrific lady,' he said. 'Mary's lucky to have her. Victoria is too. I wouldn't worry . . . look how close you and your aunt are. She's been as good as a real mom, hasn't she?'

Rose smiled, thinking of the relationship she had with her Aunt Rosa. It wasn't quite the same as Mary's situation, though. 'Aunt Rosa's wonderful. But I keep thinking of what Mary must see when she looks at Victoria,' she said. 'We see a beautiful, newborn baby girl. For Mary, this baby will always remind her of everything she's lost. Her innocence, her future. I wonder if Mary will ever be able to accept her? If, somehow, she'll hold the baby to blame?'

Ramsey didn't answer. Rose stared out the passenger window. A freight train rumbled along the track next to the interstate, barely visible in the darkness. Its speed nearly matched that of the diesel truck, but eventually the track curved away into the night. Rose thought of Mary, alone, running to find her aunt, giving birth in an odd little cabin with two complete strangers in attendance.

She glanced at Ramsey. A band of reflected light played over the lower half of his face, illuminating the healing burn across his cheek, his long, slightly crooked nose and the grim set of his lips. A muscle twitched along the side of his jaw.

'Mary's a courageous young woman.' His low voice was ragged, emotion evident in every word. 'She could have had an abortion. She didn't. She chose life for Victoria, at a great cost to herself. She's a survivor, Rose, and she'll accept her baby for what she is, a perfectly innocent child. I don't have any doubts Mary will love her little girl. She left an intolerable situation to give that child a better life. That's a frightening step for a young woman in her situation to do, but she did it out of love for her unborn baby. The time will come when Victoria understands the sacrifices her mother made for her. Believe me. I know.'

Ramsey looked briefly in Rose's direction as if challenging her to disagree, then turned back to the dark road stretching out ahead of them. Rose wondered if he was aware of the way the tears in his eyes sparkled in the pale glow of light inside the cab. Her own throat felt tight.

She couldn't reply. Couldn't explain the emotional highs and lows she'd sensed in him over the past hours, couldn't imagine what forces had shaped and molded him into such a complex creature; tough and sensitive, vulnerable and caring. A man capable of understanding a mother's sacrifice.

She watched as he clenched his jaw tightly and took a deep breath, slowly exhaling. His eyes flickered quickly in her direction, twin coals reflecting glowing embers in the darkness.

The air crackled with the charge between the two of them, a sensation so hot Rose expected sparks to flash about the darkened cab. The depth of his character stole her breath. No wonder he rarely let his emotions surface. She hadn't realized the power he kept leashed beneath the calm façade, hadn't suspected the force he held over her.

Lights from an oncoming car momentarily distracted Rose and she sucked a deep, lungful of air, wondering just how long she might have gone without breathing.

Until I passed out, most likely.

A ghost of a thought slipped through her troubled mind, that she'd never responded to any man so passionately, had never experienced the emotion, nor felt the physical need this man drew from some hidden well within her.

Had never, not ever, experienced anything remotely like this with James.

James. A man she had promised to marry. A man who had never, ever moved her as deeply, as emotionally, as sensually, as had Mike Ramsey.

Shaken by her feelings, Rose turned silently to watch the darkness speeding by outside her window.

★　★　★

Rose seemed unusually quiet tonight. Ramsey glanced in her direction, wondering if she'd sensed the powerful charge between them. She must have. That would explain the silence. It was all so damned complicated and he only had himself to blame.

He certainly hadn't expected, or wanted, this unwelcome chemistry the two of them appeared to share. Kissing Rose had been the biggest mistake he could have made. Throwing a new baby into the works hadn't helped, either. Every time he replayed the image of Rose holding the tiny newborn he felt an ache in his gut that had nothing to do with the last time he'd eaten. He suddenly wanted things he had no right to want, not if he was going to do the job he had set out to do.

At this point, he wasn't doing his job at all. In his search for the hijackers, he had essentially cut himself off from any suspects other than Rose the moment he changed the route without notifying anyone.

Even Kathleen had questioned his decision the last time they spoke, something his partner never did. How could he explain that he had to either completely exonerate Rose, or arrest her? There could be no in-between, no doubt to mar their relationship.

Relationship! Who the hell was he kidding? Where was his professionalism? Some investigator he was, traveling across country with his chief suspect. Falling in love with a woman he'd quite possibly end up throwing in jail.

Worst of all, Ramsey was nowhere closer to solving this mystery than the day he'd left Pittsburgh. So far, absolutely nothing had happened to implicate Rose. He wondered if he'd been wrong about her all along.

God, he hoped so.

★   ★   ★

'We're getting close to Cheyenne.' Ramsey stretched one arm over his head, feeling every mile they'd traveled. 'It's almost dawn. Let's

89

find a place to stop and get some rest. It's a tough haul over the Rockies.'

'Fine.' Rose flashed him a brief, pensive smile. 'I could use a shower and I need to do some laundry.'

'Running out of blue jeans, little girl?' He grinned at her, imagining her as a grass-stained tomboy in worn jeans and sneakers. Somehow, the image fit better than the look of the buttoned down executive he knew her to be. 'You country girls have a hard time staying out of the dirt, I bet.'

'Yes, actually, we do.' She smiled thoughtfully at him. 'What kind of little boy were you?' Rose shifted in her seat and leaned against the door, the better to look directly at Ramsey.

'I told you before, ornery,' Ramsey quipped, uncomfortable with the curious gleam in her eyes.

'You don't talk much about yourself, do you? Are you afraid I'll learn your secrets?' Rose's teasing voice belied the serious look on her face.

If you only knew, sweetheart. Ramsey hated the subterfuge. He wanted the job over and Rose cleared of his suspicions. He wanted Rose.

'My father ran off before I was born,' he finally said, figuring the past was safer than the present. 'My mother did her best to raise me by herself, but I was a handful. She finally remarried and my step-father straightened me out. End of story. What about you?' he asked, turning the questions away from himself. 'Tell me more about your aunt. She raised you, right?'

Curiosity about Ramsey warred with her affection for her aunt. As usual, Aunt Rosa won. Besides, Rose needed to stop thinking about James. Guilt was not a pleasant emotion. Knowing now what kind of feelings were possible between a man and woman, she couldn't believe she had agreed to be his wife. What had she been thinking?

Rose shuddered, imagining the sterile, passionless future she had barely escaped. She couldn't be angry at James, though. James had never pretended to be anyone other than who he was. He hadn't deserved the nasty way she'd ended their engagement. She needed to apologize, and soon. It wasn't his fault she didn't love him.

But she wasn't letting Ramsey off the hook all that easily, either, and she flashed him a cheeky smile to let him know she was merely *allowing* him to change the subject. 'We'll get back to you later.' She chuckled at his sheepish grin.

'Aunt Rosa's a character,' she said,

picturing her flamboyant aunt. 'She was my father's older sister. She never married, but she's certainly no 'Old Maid.' In fact, she's been having a really hot affair with her attorney for years, but she doesn't think I know about it. They're really cute together, always sneaking around when I come to visit.' Rose smiled, then pensively bit her lips. 'When my parents were killed, Aunt Rosa took me in without hesitation. Sometimes I think it was like living with a cross between Auntie Mame and Dolly Levi. She even looks like that actress, Carol Channing, and has that same scratchy, raspy voice. She runs a bed and breakfast, the Honeysuckle Inn, in the foothills near Jackson. It used to be the family home, but it's been a B and B as long as I can remember.

'I was at such a vulnerable age when my parents died, but Aunt Rosa stepped right in and wouldn't let me feel sorry for myself. I always knew I was loved, no matter what. It wasn't a conventional childhood. Nothing with Aunt Rosa could ever be called conventional.' She paused a moment, enjoying the warmth of memories, then stretched and yawned.

'Aunt Rosa's always claimed to be a bit psychic. I have to admit, sometimes she seems to speak to me when I need to hear from her . . . even when we're miles apart. It's almost like I can hear her voice in my head. I guess it's just because I miss her so much.' Rose turned and looked directly at Ramsey, wondering what he thought of her description of her eccentric aunt.

He watched her, his expression completely unreadable. 'How about you, Ramsey?' Rose asked. 'What was your childhood like?'

'Not like yours,' he grunted, turning the steering wheel and taking an exit off the freeway. 'I ran pretty wild until my mother remarried. Things changed after that.'

'Was your stepfather abusive?' Rose thought of some of Ramsey's off-the-cuff comments. An abusive childhood could explain his hesitance to talk about himself.

'No, he didn't have to be. I was a big kid. He's a little guy. Hell, the chip on my shoulder was bigger than he was. He had me convinced he was an ex-CIA agent and knew a hundred different ways to hurt me without leaving a mark. I believed him.'

'Gullible, weren't you?' Rose laughed at Ramsey's dry explanation.

'Yeah, but maybe I wanted to believe him. Who knows?' *And that's the honest truth*, Ramsey thought, pulling the rig into the park-ing lot of a quiet-looking motel. *I believed him because Handy cared enough to lie to me.*

Would Rose feel the same about Ramsey's lies when this was over? Lord, how he wished this case were settled! He stole a quick look at Rose and wondered if there'd been any more hijackings in the past twenty-four hours. And most of all, he wondered if Rose had contacted anyone about their change in route.

★ ★ ★

'The deal was, I pay for my own room,' Rose said to Ramsey's back as he jiggled the key in the lock. He chuckled quietly at the schoolmarmish tone in her voice. 'I certainly hope you've got a good excuse for insisting we share this one. And don't tell me all the other rooms are taken. The parking lot is practically empty.'

'It seemed like a good idea. This isn't the best part of town, but I like it because it's convenient to the highway and I couldn't get two rooms close to each other. This way, I won't worry about you.'

And, I can keep an eye on you. He wished he could trust his own motivation. Did he want to watch Rose because he didn't trust her, or because he couldn't bear to be away from her?

'I should have known you'd have a logical reason.' Rose grumbled as she stepped into the room ahead of Ramsey. She dropped her purse in the middle of one of the two king sized beds that filled the generically bland space and slowly looked around.

Ramsey hid his surprise at her easy acceptance of a single room. Of course, maybe it didn't matter one way or the other to Rose. Maybe she didn't feel the attraction that was slowly driving Ramsey nuts. He found that hard to believe, then wondered if his logic was controlled by male ego.

'It ain't the Desert Palm Hideaway, but I guess it'll do.' Rose's drawl was thick enough to cut with a knife.

'Now that had character,' Ramsey agreed. He flipped on more lights to illuminate the boring beige and cream-colored room. 'I'll get our bags.'

Rose merely nodded and looked away. She seemed unusually interested in the swirling brown and white pattern on the bedspread. Was she thinking of the two full days they'd spent together at that hideous Desert Palms Hideaway? They'd shared more than a room . . . they'd even shared a bed.

Thank goodness he'd been too exhausted to think about it at the time. Unfortunately, he'd thought about it a lot last night, driving across Nebraska. In fact, the image of Rose curled snugly against his chest had been uppermost in his mind as they'd pulled into the motel parking lot.

Yeah, right. It had definitely been an objective decision on his part to share a room. Disgusted with the direction his thoughts kept straying, Ramsey carried the bags inside.

Rose gestured toward the small bathroom. 'Do you want the shower first? You look absolutely exhausted.'

She, on the other hand, looked wonderful. She'd slipped her shoes off and was comfortably stretched out on the bed. Ramsey thought about stretching out next to her . . . or possibly sharing the shower. Now *that* had a certain attraction.

'Yeah,' he said, banishing the appealing fantasy from his mind. 'If you don't mind.' He stood there a moment longer, wondering at the thoughts behind those dark green eyes, remembering the taste of her lips.

She gazed back, her dark brows furrowed with unasked questions.

Mentally shaking himself, Ramsey grabbed his overnight bag off the bed and headed for the bathroom. Quickly he shut the door and leaned against it, dropping his bag to the floor.

God, he'd almost leaned over and kissed her, like it would have been the natural thing to do. He was definitely going to have to watch himself.

He'd thought about it so many times, of pulling her into his embrace, tasting her full lips and twisting her heavy length of hair through his fingers. He'd done it so often in his mind over the last couple of days, he'd almost done it in reality.

That could have been awkward.

Well, maybe not.

As long as there wasn't any Chinese food nearby.

How would she have reacted? With shock? No, considering the way she'd responded to his kiss before, she probably would have kissed him back.

He couldn't let it happen, not now, not until he knew for certain. Ramsey undressed, then adjusted the water temperature and stepped under the steaming spray. Lathering his chest and arms with the small bar of soap, he let his thoughts wander, again. As usual, they immediately returned to the kiss, to the sweet taste of Rose's lips and her tiny, whimpering moan of pleasure. Ramsey allowed the fantasy to linger for a moment before recalling the climax of their brief encounter, Rose's outraged shriek of surprise when the chicken chow mein landed in her lap.

Chuckling to himself, Ramsey rinsed off under the warm spray. That ridiculous image worked better than a cold shower every time.

★ ★ ★

Rose heard the clatter of pipes when Ramsey shut off the water, and quickly ended the phone call with James. She didn't want Ramsey to know she'd called her ex-fiancé. James was an embarrassing part of her past, something she'd just as soon forget. She certainly didn't want Ramsey to know she'd been so desperate to end her loneliness she'd agreed to marry a man she didn't love. It was too humiliating.

So was the conversation she'd just had with James.

He didn't act upset over their broken engagement, or surprised to hear, not only was she traveling with a strange man, she was also sharing his room. Had Denise told him about Ramsey and the trip to California?

If not, he should have been outraged. It didn't make sense.

Especially since she'd never spent a single night with James. Of course, he'd never

98

pressured her for a more intimate relationship. She tried to imagine how Ramsey would
react if the situation were reversed. The
thought sent a chill along her spine.

James had politely asked about her travel
plans and how long she intended to visit her
aunt. In fact, he'd been very polite. She hated
to admit how much that hurt. The least he
could have done was act a tiny bit jealous,
maybe display just a little passionate outrage.
There'd been no passion at all. None.

But, if he didn't love her any more than she
loved him, he had no reason to feel jealous.
*He doesn't love me and I don't love him. So
why did we even get engaged?* She tried to
remember if James had ever acted romantic.
He'd sent flowers on her birthday. They went
to the theater, had the occasional dinner out.
He'd been persistent but non-demanding.
He'd been . . . *comfortable.*

There was absolutely nothing comfortable
about Mike Ramsey. There'd been more
passion in Ramsey's smoldering looks than
she'd ever felt in James's lukewarm kisses. So
why had he even proposed in the first place?

Why had she accepted?

'Who were you talking to?' Ramsey stood
just inside the open bathroom door, drying
his hair with a thick, white towel.

'Uh, no one.' Rose swallowed the lie.

99

'Unless you heard me talking to myself.' No way was she going to discuss her conversation with James. It was time to put that part of her life behind her.

'I was sure I heard you on the phone.' Ramsey draped the towel around his broad shoulders and ran his fingers through his hair, slicking it back from his forehead. Dressed only in a pair of worn gray sweats riding low on his narrow hips, he looked positively threatening. He leaned against the doorjamb and folded his arms across his bare chest, watching Rose from beneath wet, spiky lashes. Studying her. After a moment, he pushed himself away from the wall, crossed the room and stretched out on the king sized bed next to Rose's. 'Guess I was mistaken. I was sure I heard you talking to someone.'

'Well, I wasn't.' He had no right to accuse her. She let him know it with her tone of voice. Okay, so maybe she shouldn't lie to him, but it was too late to change her story, now. She'd look even more foolish and she'd end up telling him about her stupid engagement to James and he'd know she was a complete idiot. It was bad enough feeling that way herself.

Besides, her conversation with James was private and personal, not any of Ramsey's business. What gave him the right to interrogate her?

The fact there's obviously something between us. The fact I lied. The fact I care what he thinks. Her skin felt hot. Damn, she was blushing. She'd never been able to get away with a fib, but Ramsey didn't know that. With any luck, he'd think she was just angry. Rising stiffly from the bed, Rose turned her back on Ramsey and headed for the bathroom. 'It's my turn in the shower.'

'Whatever you say.' Ramsey's voice held an angry edge, his eyes were dark pinpoints of hostile light. 'Whatever you say.'

★ ★ ★

'She's in the shower, Kathleen, but she's made contact with someone . . . No, I don't know who, and she's not about to tell me. Probably put the call on her credit card. I saw her wallet out on the desk. I guess my hunch was right after all. Exactly. If she weren't acting guilty as hell, I wouldn't think she had something to hide. I want you to check the phone records. See what you can find. Get a warrant if you have to. I want to know who she talked to. Find out what you can, then get your butt out to Salt Lake, same place we stayed before. Then follow us on in to Nevada

. . . near Reno, I think. I'm convinced that stolen equipment was moved south, down to Yerington or even out toward Fallon. The desert has a lot of hiding places. I'm guessing that's where they'll hit us. Just a hunch. Thanks, I'm sorry, too. I was hoping I was wrong.'

Ramsey set the phone back in its cradle. Disappointment coursed through him in heated waves, then settled into a painful lump in the middle of his gut. He rubbed his hand roughly across his jaw line, then kneaded the stiff muscles at the base of his neck before stretching out on the bed.

He tried to work through different scenarios, each one designed to prove Rose's innocence. Maybe she was calling that Aunt Rosa of hers and didn't like him snooping. The only problem was, he had a really bad feeling about the phone call, and he had no doubt she'd made one.

What he didn't know added up to a hell of a lot more than what he did know. He wanted proof Rose was innocent. He wanted to be wrong on this one.

It looked as if the only way he'd find out for sure was if they made it to California without a hijacking.

He hoped Kathleen could come up with a name on Rose's phone call, a name of someone totally uninvolved in this mess. If this turned out to be a wild goose chase it would be worth every sarcastic insult his partner was certain to throw at him. He'd never wanted to be wrong so much in his life.

'Something's just not right,' he muttered. He pushed himself upright, leaned against the headboard and sighed deeply. His thoughts swirled without direction. He'd just have to keep hoping she wasn't involved in the thefts, even when everything pointed to her guilt.

Except for one very important thing. Thieves have to be good liars. Rose isn't. Ramsey sat up a little straighter on the bed. Rose DeAngelo couldn't lie worth beans and hope to get away with it.

For some reason she lied to me about making a phone call, but lying's not something Rose does very often, that's for sure. If she had any idea at all how expressive that gorgeous face of hers is, she'd never tell a lie, again. She's not a thief, or the whole world would know it.

Smiling at his sudden insight, Ramsey settled back against the pillows, but he couldn't ignore the little voice telling him he was in pretty deep, if that was all it took to convince him of Rose's innocence.

★ ★ ★

Rose managed to stay mad at Ramsey all the way through her shower, but when she stepped out of the warm bathroom and saw him stretched out on the bed, her anger melted away.

By all rights she was the one who should apologize. She'd lied to him. But it was obvious from the way he was staring at her that an apology was the last thing on his mind.

The towel she'd wrapped around herself covered her from above her breasts to just below her thighs, but Ramsey's fervent look left her feeling naked. 'I left my bag out here,' she mumbled through suddenly dry lips. 'Could you hand it to me, please?'

'I'm resting.' He shrugged his shoulders in a helpless gesture and grinned. 'Why don't you come get it yourself?'

Her bag was on the far side of the bed, tucked between the wall and his legs. She'd have to reach over Ramsey to grab it. From the lecherous grin on his face, there was no doubt what he was thinking.

He had to be thinking the same as she. Of the two of them locked in a passionate embrace, her towel falling away beneath his searching, stroking hands, his lips taking hers in a searing kiss. *Damn!* Rose felt the hot flush spread across her throat and face. Why hadn't she felt this way about James? At least he'd wanted to marry her. Marriage was obviously the last thing on Ramsey's mind. She took a step back.

'What's the matter?' he asked. 'Don't you trust me?'

Rose glared at him, then tugged the towel tighter across her breasts. Trust had nothing to do with it. She just didn't know what he wanted from her. Gingerly she placed one knee on the bed and leaned across Ramsey's legs, fully expecting his strong arm to snake out and grab her. She grasped the handle on the bag and pulled it across his thighs, backing away from the bed so quickly she bumped into the other mattress with the backs of her knees. He hadn't tried a thing. Pressing her lips together, she spun around and headed toward the bathroom to dress.

'Rose.'

She turned slowly at his soft command, her fingers twisting in the towel she clutched against her breasts.

'I'll never hurt you,' he said, all humor gone from his eyes. 'Not if I can help it. You'll have to trust me.'

'I don't understand.' He confused her even when he wasn't being cryptic. The conflicting emotions evident in his shadowed eyes didn't give her a clue to what he was thinking, now.

'Is there some reason I shouldn't trust you?'

He answered her question with one of his own. 'Can I trust you, Rose?'

'Of course.' She didn't even try to disguise her bewilderment. What exactly was going on behind that intense, gray-eyed gaze of his? Why all this talk about trust? Maybe he *was* an axe murderer!

Right. She'd only known Mike Ramsey for a few days, but she was certain of one thing. He was not a criminal.

'I need to be sure,' he said, then looked away.

Rose frowned, more perplexed than ever. She started to speak, took a deep breath instead, and escaped into the safety of the bathroom.

6

Friday morning, Wyoming

Rose frowned at her reflection in the steamy mirror. What had gotten into the man? Just when she thought she'd figured Ramsey out, he went and turned all her feelings upside down, inside out and backwards.

She ran her fingertips across her full lower lip and tried to recall the teasing character of Ramsey's kiss from so many days ago. Why hadn't he kissed he, again? And why that strange conversation about trust? He made no sense. None whatsoever.

Of course he could trust her. The only fib she'd told him was about that stupid phone call, and James was none of his business. For that matter, how much did she know about Mike Ramsey?

Not a damned thing, really. Maybe she was the one who should worry about trust.

Rose sighed, shaking her head in complete bewilderment. So much had happened over the past few days, but none of it made sense. It would, though, once she made it home and got a dose of her aunt's pragmatic advice and earthy humor. She needed a long chat over a glass of good wine to help her figure everything out. Especially her feelings for Ramsey.

She'd never been so physically attracted to a man in her life. It couldn't possibly be love. She didn't want it to be love. She'd just ended one pathetic relationship, she certainly didn't need another.

If only Ramsey weren't so damned sexy.

Rose towel-dried her damp hair, then carefully worked through the snarls with a plastic brush. When one particularly troublesome knot refused to come free, she propped her hip against the counter while she worked on it. As her fingers worked against the snarls, Rose's mind wandered. What would happen if she asked Ramsey to help her untangle the damp strands?

He'd be there in a heartbeat. She could almost feel those long, supple fingers of his working their way across her scalp, lifting the heavy weight of hair and carefully combing the tangles. He'd leave it sleek and smooth across her shoulders, maybe even plant a soft kiss in that sensitive spot behind her ear when he was through.

She sighed, indulging a moment longer in her fantasy.

And to think James had wanted her to cut it all off.

Short hair might be more sophisticated, but she'd certainly never fantasized James's precise, well-manicured hands playing with her imaginary, stylishly trimmed curls.

In fact, she'd never fantasized about James at all.

Damn Mike Ramsey and his sexy good looks. Damn his strong, capable hands and his broad shoulders and dark gray eyes with the velvet lashes. She didn't need him in her life and she'd be damned if she wanted him in her heart.

Rose tugged her clean, flannel gown on over her head, then quickly tied her damp hair into a loose ponytail, sighing once again as she took another quick look in the steamy mirror. She could cuss all she wanted, but whether she liked it or not, Mike Ramsey was currently very much a part of her life.

And as much as she feared the idea, Rose knew he already owned a piece of her heart.

She walked out into the room, wishing she'd added a bathrobe to her new wardrobe. The warm flannel gown covered her from throat to toes, but the king-sized beds suddenly looked much closer together and Ramsey's naked torso and lean hips were much too attractive.

'We need to figure out what to do for dinner.'

Damn him. Her heart was doing double-time over his bare chest, and all Ramsey wanted to discuss was food. Would she ever understand him?

Rose dug through the promotional materials in the top drawer of the bedside table, searching for menus to local restaurants. It was easier than looking at Ramsey, especially in his current state of dress.

The ringing cellular phone on the table in front of her startled Rose and she snatched it up without thinking. Ramsey's shoulders tensed and his hands stilled at the sound. He must have been expecting a call. Why else would he have brought the phone in from the truck when there was a perfectly good phone in the room? It beeped again.

Curiosity won out. Rose answered it.

The silky female voice on the line startled her. Why hadn't she even considered Ramsey might have a woman in his life? A man as handsome and intelligent as he . . . 'Just a moment,' she said, unwilling to make eye contact with him as she handed over the phone and stepped back. She heard Ramsey's soft 'hello' behind her, grabbed her coat, and headed for the door.

Ramsey covered the mouthpiece on the phone. 'Where are you going?' he demanded.

'Outside. I thought you might like some

privacy for your conversation.'

'There's no need for that. I'll just be a minute.' Ramsey put the phone to his ear and turned his back. Rose felt as if she'd just been dismissed.

She reached around Ramsey and grabbed the stack of papers she'd been looking at, then settled on the opposite bed to sort through them.

Ramsey quickly ended the call and set the phone next to Rose on the bed. 'If Kathleen calls back, holler, would you? I need to go out and check some things on the truck. I'm not really all that hungry. How about if I just grab something at the bakery next door? Would that be enough for you?'

'That would be fine,' Rose said, putting the menus aside. Suddenly she wasn't very hungry, either.

Ramsey reached for his jacket and slipped it on over his bare chest.

'Who's Kathleen?' Rose asked, unable to contain her interest. Ramsey flashed her a cheeky grin and Rose wished she could retract the question. Except she really wanted to know.

'Nosy, aren't we?' Ramsey headed toward the door. Rose felt the telltale flush rising across her collarbones. She wished Ramsey would just hurry up and leave. Instead, he paused near the door. She heard him grab the handle and knew he watched her. She felt his gaze boring into her, but she refused to raise her eyes in his direction.

'She's a friend from work. Just a very good friend.' In the long silence that followed Ramsey's clipped explanation, Rose was certain she heard her own heartbeat. There were all kinds of friends. She flashed back to his comments about trust.

'We're not involved. Never have been. Don't plan to be.'

Ramsey's soft words hung between them for a moment, words that told Rose more than she had expected to hear and exactly what she'd hoped he might say. She raised her head, turning her full attention on the man gazing so intently back at her.

She had the uncanny feeling their relationship had just shifted gears. It was there again, that sense of waiting, the feeling of contact without touch, of awareness bordering on understanding. Rose licked her lips, wondered how to respond, finally settled on a simple, 'Oh.'

Ramsey grinned, tipped an imaginary hat, then turned and went out the door. Rose stared after him, scared to death she'd gone and fallen in love. *No*, she thought. *Impossible. Absolutely, unequivocally impossible.*

He'd only been gone a couple of minutes when the phone beeped again. Sighing, Rose picked it up, fully expecting Kathleen's silky voice.

Aunt Rosa's warm greeting and raucous laughter brought an answering chuckle from Rose. 'Aunt Rosa, it's so good to hear your voice.' She was still laughing at Rosa's silly comments when Ramsey stepped into the room almost fifteen minutes later. Rose gestured to Ramsey as he quietly closed the door.

'Is it Kathleen?' he asked, taking the phone from her outstretched hand, at the same time setting a heavenly smelling bakery box down on the bed next to Rose.

'No, it's Aunt Rosa. I want you to meet her.'

'Hello Aunt Rosa,' Ramsey said, grinning down at Rose as she lifted the lid off the box and inhaled the warm scent of freshly baked pastries. His smile quickly faded. He held the phone away from his ear and ended the call. 'No one there,' he said. 'We must have been cut off.'

'That's weird.' Rose's mouth watered from the luscious smells. 'We had a really clear connection. In fact, let me know how much I owe you for that call, because it's going to be expensive! We gabbed a long time. You never should have let me give Aunt Rosa your private number!' She grabbed a warm apple fritter and took a big bite. '*Mmmmm*. This is heavenly.' She scooted back against the headboard, taking the bakery box with her. 'If you're nice, I'll share.'

Rose's look of sensual pleasure as she chewed the warm pastry clouded Ramsey's thoughts. He should be wondering about the phone call, not the expression of uninhibited rapture on her face. How could he be sure she'd really been talking to her aunt?

Rose maintained constant contact with the woman, or so she said. Could Aunt Rosa be a code name for the thieves? Rose licked a tiny crumb from the corner of her full lips. Ramsey tried, and failed, to form a cohesive thought. He'd worry about Aunt Rosa, later.

He chuckled quietly. Exhaustion had dulled his senses to everything and everyone but Rose. How the hell had he gotten himself into this mess? How was he going to get out?

Kathleen's quick check of the phone records hadn't turned up a thing. It would take at least a couple of days before the information was available, since the motel was connected to a small, private phone company. In the meantime, was it all that wrong to let himself believe in Rose's innocence?

He'd thought about it the whole time she was in the shower. She'd lied about the phone call, but that didn't necessarily mean she was guilty of running a gang of hijackers.

Rose was innocent. She had to be. She was too caring and compassionate and too damned honest, if her lack of skill at lying told him anything. She couldn't be a thief.

Unless he counted the way she'd stolen his heart.

Thinking along those lines was bound to get him into trouble. Spending the past few days in a state of suspended lust must have addled his brain.

Ramsey yawned, stretching his arms above his head to work out the tired muscles. There was an audible crackling sound as he twisted his back and leaned over to touch his toes.

'You must be exhausted.' Rose sipped her cup of steaming coffee, glanced at him, then looked away. If only he could read her mind.

'Would a back rub help you sleep?'

'Are you serious?' Didn't she have any idea how much he wanted her? A montage of provocative images suddenly crowded his mind at the thought of Rose's long legs straddling his buttocks, her silky hair brushing his tired muscles as she pressed herself along him to knead and pummel his shoulders.

When she nodded in agreement, Ramsey could barely stammer his reply. 'Um, yeah, a back rub would feel really good.' Was she kidding? As if he'd even consider rejecting her offer!

'Lie down,' she ordered. Ramsey didn't question her sudden change of heart, just obediently stretched out on the bed. To his vast disappointment, Rose knelt next to him on the bedspread instead of straddling his hips.

'I use this lotion after a workout,' she said, pouring something cool along his spine and filling the air with an aromatic mixture of lavender, honeysuckle, mint and camphor.

She had strong hands for a woman, strong hands and long, supple fingers. She knew exactly which muscles to knead, how much pressure to apply. Ramsey didn't even try to control his groans of pleasure.

Her long hair, tied in a loose ponytail, hung over her left shoulder. The damp length of it swept along his ribs as she moved, its coolness a direct contrast to the heat from her hands.

She worked along his spine, kneading the lotion into his sore muscles. Her touch was pure magic, easing the stiffness and tightness with each caress.

Unfortunately, the one part of him she

neglected to stroke was uncomfortably stiff. In his benumbed state, Ramsey thought of asking Rose if she'd consider a more thorough massage, but felt too relaxed to form the words. Besides, even the ache of his arousal couldn't counteract Rose's healing touch.

She hummed quietly while she worked, smoothing and easing away the pain of long miles behind the wheel, of long hours contemplating all the reasons Mike Ramsey was wrong for Rose DeAngelo. Years of loneliness, a lifetime of questions, all melted and flowed into insignificance as her fingers stroked and kneaded and healed.

Somewhere between his lats and trapezius muscles, Ramsey drifted off to sleep, his mind filled with the scent of honeysuckle and the sound of Rose, softly humming *Amazing Grace*.

★ ★ ★

'Ramsey. Ramsey, wake up.'

'I don' wanna,' he mumbled, rubbing his face into the pillow. He couldn't have shut his eyes for more than a few minutes. How come Rose had stopped rubbing his back? He couldn't remember a back rub feeling so good. 'Why'd ya quit?' he muttered, rolling

117

over and squinting his eyes.

'One, because you fell asleep, and two, because I don't give twelve-hour back rubs. It's almost eight p.m., you lazy bum.'

'Twelve hours? It can't be!' How could he have slept so long? Had she contacted anyone? Ramsey pulled himself into a sitting position and tucked the blankets around his hips. He didn't even remember climbing under the covers.

'Yes, it can be.' She stood next to the bed, hands on hips, head cocked to one side. Her words might be brisk and teasing, but the look on her face was oddly vulnerable. 'I've been awake for ages and I'm tired of watching you sleep,' she said. 'I'm packed and ready to go. Maybe I should just leave without you.' She grinned and held her hand out to him.

Ramsey shook his head in a vain attempt to clear his fogged brain. 'That must have been some back rub, unless you slipped a Mickey in my coffee. I never sleep more than six hours, seven, max.'

'Magic fingers.' Rose waggled her fingers under his nose. 'C'mon. You must have needed the sleep, Ramsey. Admit you wear out once in awhile, that you need rest just like all us other mere mortals.' She grabbed his hand to pull him out of bed.

'I can't afford to wear out,' Ramsey said.

'It's not on my schedule.' Rose grinned in reply and tightened her grasp on his hand. He wrapped his fingers just as tightly around hers and fought an overwhelming urge to pull her down onto the bed with him. Would it be so awful to give in once to a human weakness?

The lost hours while he'd slept filled Ramsey's mind with a new set of worries. He let Rose tug him upright.

They were definitely way behind schedule. He needed to check in with Kathleen and he wanted to make Salt Lake by morning. They still had to stop for dinner. Had Rose called anyone while he blissfully slept the day away? Groaning, Ramsey dragged himself out of bed and headed for the bathroom. When had his life become so complicated?

The answer was obvious: the day he rescued Rose DeAngelo.

★　★　★

It was almost nine by the time they reached Laramie. A rosy glow in the western sky marked the end of the day and for the first time Rose truly regretted the fact they traveled at night. The huge granite mountains and thick pine forests were merely dark silhouettes in the evening sky, soon lost in the

119

garish light from the truck stop Ramsey pulled into off the freeway.

Ramsey climbed out of the cab while Rose scrambled out on her side to meet him on the ground. 'I would have helped you down if you'd waited,' he said. The impatient edge to his voice surprised her.

'C'mon.' He headed across the parking lot. When she didn't immediately follow, he stopped, turned, smiled apologetically and held his hand out to her.

Rose hesitated, suddenly awash with a sense of how easy it could be to fall in love with this man in spite of his odd moods, his unpredictable ways.

No, dammit! Absolutely not. It was physical attraction, pure and simple. She was a healthy woman in her prime and he was a healthy man. So healthy he took her breath away. Rose licked her lips, then tentatively placed her hand in his. His grip was certain, strong, the callused fingers warm.

Together they walked across the dark parking lot. There was no denying the attraction between them. She knew he felt it as well as she. He just seemed to hide it a little better, deal with it more efficiently. She couldn't help but admire his control.

What wasn't there to like about Ramsey? His toughness tempered by vulnerability, his strong, sensitive hands and the way his jeans molded his firm buttocks.

Already she could recognize that loose, sexy walk of his anywhere and that recognition gave her a sense of possession she had no right to feel.

Well, she was going to feel it anyway. When he looked directly into her eyes and grinned, or ran his fingers through his hair while deep in thought, or did any of a hundred little things that had become familiar, Rose felt almost as if she owned those private gestures that were intrinsically his.

It couldn't be love. Rose lengthened her stride to keep up with Ramsey. Whatever it was, she felt it, felt it deep inside where she'd never experienced such feelings before. *Lust?* That must be it. Lust she could deal with.

Ignore it long enough, it'd go away. That shouldn't be too difficult. As long as Ramsey didn't find out how she felt. He wasn't the type to settle down, she'd figured that out almost immediately, but it was obvious he wouldn't turn down a chance at a little cross-country fling.

Definitely not a good idea to let him know how she felt.

That was not the way Rose DeAngelo worked. Never had. Never would. No way would she let Mike Ramsey know she'd like nothing more than to jump his bones.

Sighing with the profound image brought on by that tantalizing thought, Rose took a deep breath and walked beside Ramsey, past the heavy glass door into the brightly lit cafe.

7

Friday evening, Laramie, Wyoming

Rose pushed limp pieces of lettuce around the plate, her appetite fading with the growing realization of how deeply involved she'd become with the man sitting quietly across the table from her.

Monday it had all sounded so simple. Hitch a ride with the good looking hero who'd saved her life and go to California to visit Aunt Rosa. Well, here she sat, five days later, staring at a wilted salad in a cheap little diner in Wyoming, worrying about a serious case of what she hoped was lust, but had all the signs of heartbreak.

'Had enough?' Ramsey's soft question broke into her thoughts.

'Yeah. How about you? Was your steak okay?'

'I've had better. C'mon. Let's hit the road.'

Pushing her uneaten salad aside, Rose left her portion of the tab on the table with Ramsey's and followed him outside.

Ramsey checked the tie-downs on the load, but his thoughts were on Rose and her unusually quiet behavior. Something had upset her, but he had no idea what was going through her mind. Hell, sometimes he wondered what was going through his own.

What a week. He was no closer to solving this case than he'd been a month ago, his delivery to Sacramento was already overdue and he was saddled with a serious case of unrequited lust for his prime suspect.

There was no excuse for the predicament he'd gotten himself into. Kathleen had accused him of losing his objectivity, of letting his undercover investigation deteriorate into a cross-country date with his chief suspect.

She was absolutely right.

He'd been lusting after Rose like a teenager after his first kiss. Except once he'd gotten that kiss, he wanted more.

But he couldn't have her. Rose struck him as the forever type. Definitely not his style. Even if it was, he had to accept the fact there was absolutely no chance for the two of them. When this was all over, Rose would hate him. He couldn't see any way to avoid it. If she were guilty he'd be the one putting handcuffs on her. If she were innocent . . . Lord, the minute she found out he was investigating the hijackings, she'd know she'd been a suspect all along.

She'd know the Mike Ramsey she thought she knew was a fraud.

Intimacy required trust. Ramsey thought of the conversation he'd had with Rose. He'd had no right to ask her to trust him. He sure as hell didn't trust her. He glanced in the direction of the diner, at the phone booth illuminated under a strong light. At Rose, supposedly calling her aunt. He wondered who she was really talking to.

'No trust, no relationship, period,' he muttered. Time to cool things with Rose. It was the only way.

★　★　★

Ramsey steered the big rig out onto the freeway. Rose sat as close to the door as she could, as far from him as possible. Since this was what he wanted, why did her subtle rejection hurt so much? 'Did you get hold of your aunt?' He watched her expression out of the corner of his eye. He wanted to take that worried frown off her face, he wanted . . .

Hell. He didn't know what he wanted.

'No, and the answering machine wasn't on, either. I hope she's okay. I probably should have called her back after we got cut off this morning.'

'As I recall, you were deeply involved with

a hot apple fritter.' He winked at Rose. She snorted, then flashed him a cheeky, heart-melting grin. The tension in the cab faded like a wisp of old smoke. Ramsey's good intentions flew out the window. How could he cool things with Rose when everything she did made him hot?

'It's Friday night. She's probably out with her poker group,' Rose said. 'She's never home if there's a card game in town.'

'She sounds like a neat lady.' *If she's for real. Damn.* Would he always have to question Rose's honesty?

'Everyone loves Rosa. They can't help it.' Rose seemed to relax more into her corner of the cab. 'I always wanted to be like her. She epitomizes a true *joie de vivre*. Nothing fazes her. She's nothing like me. I worry about everything.'

'Someone's got to.' Ramsey glanced at Rose. She wore her jeans tonight, and the forest green sweatshirt over her plaid western shirt. She blended into the shadows in her dark clothing, but her face reflected the pale glow from the lights on the dash. Her eyes gleamed with their own fire.

'I hope so,' she finally said, 'because I'm good at it. With the least amount of effort, I can turn normal, everyday things into major problems. Look what I managed to do with a quiet ride in the country. The original intent was to work off stress. Now, here I am in a diesel truck somewhere in Wyoming with a very kind knight in shining armor who could probably lose his job for helping me. Definitely not a stress-free situation. You should be worried, too,' she deadpanned.

'You're the expert, you handle it,' Ramsey replied. *Talk about stress*, he wanted to shout. If she only knew.

'Be glad to. I just want you to know I really am sorry for the way I messed up your schedule.'

'Don't be. It's not all your fault. Damsel rescuing's a snap, even protecting muggers from damsels isn't much, but delivering babies'll put you behind every time.' He sighed dramatically. 'We knights have to expect it. Comes with the territory.' The husky sound of her laughter burst out of the darkness and skittered along his nerves.

Intentions be damned. If ever there was a woman he shouldn't want, it was Rose. Somehow, he had to get past this adolescent need for her so he could think straight.

Unfortunately, the best solution to a healthy case of lust was out of the question. That didn't mean he couldn't dream about it, though. Where Rose was concerned, his imagination was proving to be quite vivid.

'I certainly didn't plan to cause you this much trouble.' Rose's soft words snapped Ramsey out of his fantasy and back into the conversation. 'But Aunt Rosa always said life's what happens while you're making plans.'

'She's right. Life happens,' he quipped. 'Scary thing is, I think I'm getting used to it.' They laughed together.

God, she was beautiful. She couldn't possibly be involved in this mess.

He checked the rearview mirror, just in case.

There was no one behind them.

Would he ever be able to trust her? 'Actually,' he said, putting that worry aside for the moment, 'I'm glad you were along, or I might have had to deliver that baby by myself. Thanks but no thanks.'

'That was quite an experience, wasn't it?'

'It sure was. And not one I care to repeat, thank you.'

'Even with your own children?'

His own children?

Her innocent question suddenly opened up whole worlds, a universe of possibilities, a future he'd never considered.

'I never thought about it,' he said, surprised by the surge of emotions her question raised. 'I've never considered having a family.'

Ramsey glanced at Rose, wondering. Did he even dare think beyond this case?

Possibilities, hell. More like impossibilities.

Who'd he think he was kidding? Just himself. No matter how this case ended, he'd already ruined any chance for the two of them to have a future together. She didn't strike him as a woman who'd forgive easily.

God, what a mess!

A mess that was his fault, not hers.

Unless she was guilty. *Damn!*

Even worse, while he was falling in lust, it sounded like Rose might be falling in love. He hadn't done anything to discourage her feelings for him. In fact he'd kissed her, let her think he cared for her.

Because he did. He cared about her a lot.

But it wasn't love. Definitely not love.

Definitely a mess. One only he had the power to fix.

'You have to settle down if you want a family,' he said, watching that universe of possibilities disappear into a bottomless black hole. 'I like my life on the road too much to tie myself down with a wife and kids.'

'Oh. I guess I just assumed, I mean, you seemed like such a natural with Victoria.'

'When you have your own, you're stuck with 'em. Mary's baby was just that, Mary's baby. No, I don't see myself as father material. That requires marriage, in my book, and marriage is definitely out of the question.' He took a deep breath, struggling to control the passionate surge of anger sweeping over him. He didn't want to say these things! He was throwing it all away, any chance at that normal life he'd glimpsed.

He looked at Rose. She turned away from him.

Ramsey checked the road, then glanced back at Rose. Headlights from an oncoming truck reflected off the smooth line of her jaw and tightly compressed lips. Obviously he'd made her angry with his flip reply.

Wasn't that exactly what he'd wanted?

Ramsey struggled with the need to apologize, to explain. It would only make things worse. Let her think what he'd led her to believe. Let her believe a lie, that he didn't look at her and dream of tomorrows.

Ramsey checked his speed, then backed off a little. They were nearing the Continental Divide, driving through a wide expanse of high, flat terrain. They'd passed Walcott and Fort Steele and the darkness here was absolute.

Except for the headlights reflecting off the rearview mirror.

A trucker's load had been hijacked near here less than a month ago. Ramsey checked the rearview mirror again. The lights behind them gained steadily. He reached under the dash to find the panic button, the device that would signal his partner, then glanced at Rose. She appeared totally unaware of the vehicle following them.

Appearances aren't always . . . and all that stuff.

Ramsey down-shifted, dividing his attention between the rapidly closing headlights and the silent woman beside him. Was this all part of a set up? Her silence, her talk of children, the subtle scent of honeysuckle and lavender teasing his senses? Was all of it skillfully designed to take his mind off the job? The diesel crested a small hill. The lights following them briefly disappeared, only to reappear directly behind the rig.

Ramsey glanced at Rose. She sat quietly, barely visible in the pale lights from the dashboard. Even in the dim light he knew she was angry. Angry because of him.

She was upset because he'd led her to believe he wasn't the man she wanted him to be. It was true, wasn't it? He wasn't anything close to what she thought he was . . . and maybe she wasn't who he suspected her to be, either.

Ramsey blocked thoughts of Rose and turned his attention to the speeding vehicle moving up to pass him on the left. Was this the point where the thieves cut across in front, jack-knifing his rig? Would they risk their leader's safety? Would he see the long barrel of a gun pointing directly at him, as one of the victims had described?

His shoulders tensed as the vehicle matched the pace of the big rig, hovering in the blind spot just off to his left. He slowed a bit, allowing the driver more of an opportunity to pass, then blinked, momentarily blinded by the bright headlights reflected in his side mirror.

He glanced down as the mini-van swept by, then sighed, almost giddy with relief. His pursuers were nothing more than a family, a man and a woman in front and three little kids in the back two seats. One of the little boys grinned and waved as the family van passed the big diesel and pulled safely around in front.

Ramsey watched the taillights as the van pulled away, then rolled his shoulders to relieve the tension of the past few minutes. Rose shifted her position but didn't speak. Thank goodness she had no idea what he'd been thinking.

'I apologize,' Rose said, finally breaking the silence. 'I don't know what I'm thinking. I have no right to be angry with you, and I

. . . I'm sorry for assuming things about you . . . I have no right . . . I . . . I guess it's just that I always thought I'd have a husband and children by now, and here I am, thirty years old and somehow it just hasn't happened that way. I mean, a week ago I was thinking about planning my wedding . . . ' Her voice trailed off, but Ramsey couldn't miss the little catch in her voice.

'Life happens,' Ramsey said dryly, repeating his earlier quip. He wished he knew more about her failed engagement.

'Does it ever.' Rose laughed gently. 'I . . . well . . . ' She paused, biting her lower lip, and Ramsey was certain she blushed. 'Traveling with you, catching that little purse snatcher, helping to deliver Mary's baby . . . it's been a pretty emotional week, and much too easy to pretend,' she added in a rush. 'It's not your fault I've got a good imagination. I apologize.'

So she had been thinking about him. He'd been right, after all, and now she'd given him the perfect opportunity to make his position clear. Still, he had to clear his throat twice to get the words out.

'You're young, Rose.' It was a struggle to keep his voice light. 'It'll happen. You just need to find the right man.'

'You're right. I know you're right,' she said,

her voice sounding much like Ramsey's. Forced brevity was difficult to disguise. 'I guess it's just really embarrassing, you know, getting caught in a fantasy?' Her laughter definitely sounded forced. 'Everything will work out just fine. I have to stop worrying about things I can't change.' She smiled brightly, too brightly, then quickly looked away, ending the conversation.

'Yeah,' he muttered. 'Ya gotta quit worrying about those things you can't change.'

★　★　★

They dropped down out of the mountains at dawn, Saturday. Salt Lake City sprawled before them like a garden oasis on the edge of the Great Salt Lake. Rose insisted on her own room and Ramsey agreed. He didn't tell Rose that the attractive blond in the room between them was his partner, Kathleen Malone. Nor did he tell Rose her phone was bugged.

Ramsey stepped out of the shower just as three light taps sounded on the connecting door. He was still tucking the towel around his waist when the unlocked door opened. His partner stepped into the motel room.

'Good to see you, big guy.' Kathleen reached up and patted him on the cheek, then hiked her skirt up and sat on the edge of the single king-sized bed that dominated the room. She wore black leather boots with three-inch heels, a very short, tight, black skirt and a black knit top that accentuated her sleek curves and pale blond hair. Ramsey thought she looked like a classy hooker, which was probably the image she was after.

'Rose is asleep,' she said. 'I figured it was as good a time as any to talk. By the way, you look like hell.'

'You don't.' Ramsey grinned and tweaked her on her nose, then grabbed his sweats out of the overnight bag lying on the bed next to Kathleen. He stepped back into the bathroom to dress. The light sound of her laughter followed him.

'I never do,' she said.

Ramsey snorted in agreement. No matter what they were doing, Kathleen Malone remained unruffled and gorgeous. He often thought it would have been so much easier if he could've just fallen in love with her. Tall, beautiful, tough as nails, she should have been his perfect soulmate.

That was the problem. She was too perfect a match, too much like him. So much alike, other than looks, they'd finally decided they probably had matching DNA. They'd agreed, after one tentative kiss almost five years ago, that a relationship between the two of them would be too much like incest.

It made for a perfect partnership, but a lonely social life. He'd never been able to convince another woman he could work day and night with Kathleen and keep the relationship platonic.

The only consolation was the knowledge that Kathleen's success with romance wasn't any better than his. 'So, what do you think?' he asked, drying his hair with a towel and sprawling across the bed next to Kathleen. 'Is she guilty?'

'Oh, I think she's involved,' Kathleen said, scooting up to lean against the headboard next to Ramsey. 'But I don't think she's guilty.'

'Say again?' Ramsey sat up, trying to read Kathleen's guileless blue eyes. 'How can she be involved and still be innocent?'

'I'm not sure. We're missing something, Ramsey. Something so obvious it's staring us right in the face and we're both too dumb to see it.' Kathleen swung her long legs over the side of the bed. She leaned her left elbow on her nylon clad knee and rested her chin on the knuckles of her right hand.

'You remind me of that statue, Rodin's *The Thinker*, in drag,' Ramsey said, patting her on the shoulder. 'You're cute when you're confused.'

'Help me out here, Ramsey. It's your love life I'm trying to save.'

'I haven't got a love life, Kathleen. You of all people should know.'

'You're in love with our little suspect in the next room,' she said, turning to face him. 'Don't deny it, sweetheart. I know you too well.'

'It's unrequited lust, Kat, pure and simple.' Ramsey pushed himself away from the bed then pivoted around, daring Kathleen to argue with him.

She laughed, then sighed dramatically. 'Oh Ramsey, Ramsey, Ramsey,' she intoned. 'Whatever am I gonna do with you? Denial is not a river in Egypt. I've seen you in lust, many times, requited and otherwise. This is love. You're going to have to deal with it.'

'What good's it gonna do? Answer me that,' he demanded, grabbing her shoulders for emphasis. Damn Kathleen for forcing the issue! 'If she's guilty, she goes to jail. If she's innocent, you'll probably have to arrest her for murder, because she'll kill me when she finds out she's my only suspect. There's no way out of this, Kat.' He backed away and drove both hands through his hair in frustration. 'I'm damned if she is and damned if she isn't.'

'Not necessarily, but we'll worry about

your woman later,' Kathleen said, suddenly all business. 'I managed to get the records on that phone call. Would you believe she called James Dearborn? Any reason she wouldn't tell you she'd just had a little chit-chat with her very wealthy ex-fiancé?'

'Dearborn? That's who she called?' Ramsey let out a quiet sigh of relief. 'That's okay, then. I can understand her not wanting to talk about a conversation with a guy when he'd just dumped her. She was probably too embarrassed, especially if she was trying to patch things up and couldn't.'

'That's not the way it happened, from what I learned,' Kathleen said. 'The word is, Ms. DeAngelo decided to end the engagement and stuck about twenty-five thousand dollars worth of diamond ring in Dearborn's pocket on her way out the door at Acme. Did it in front of his mother and an office full of fellow employees.' Kathleen started laughing and had to wipe her eyes before she could go on. 'Ramsey, I must admit I like her style. I guess that snotty old Alicia Dearborn just about had a stroke. Wish I could have seen it. I met that woman at a charity function last year and she gives the word *bitch* a whole new definition.'

'Rose broke it off? I'll be damned.' Ramsey plopped down on the bed next to Kathleen.

Suddenly he didn't feel nearly as exhausted as he had a few moments before. 'So, what do you make of it? Was the call important?'

'I don't know. Dearborn's an odd duck, kind of flaky, plays golf twice a week with his therapist. He's handsome, personable enough. As far as I can tell, the only work he does is to manage Mommy's sizable assets, which, of course, will one day all be his.'

'I'd like to be that odd,' Ramsey said, only half joking. What could he offer Rose to compete with James Dearborn? And she'd turned him down.

'Like I said, I think Rose is okay. You've gotten this far without a problem . . . other than a brief layover to deliver a baby,' she added, punching him on the arm. 'How'd that feel? Got the baby blues yet? Make you want a few of your own?'

She might be teasing, but Ramsey was certain he detected a wistful quality in Kathleen's words. She had to be his age, at least thirty-four. Her biological clock had a more rigid timetable than his ever would.

'Right,' he snorted. 'Can you see me with a wife and kids?'

'Yeah, Ramsey, actually I can.' Kathleen's steady gaze was soul-searchingly deep.

'I don't know, kid. I just don't know.' He sighed, then cleared his throat. 'Now get outta here. I need some sleep.'

'I'll follow until you make final delivery.' Kathleen brushed the hem of her short skirt down as she stood to leave. 'I'll check the panic button under the dash, make sure the contact's good. Do you have your weapon?'

'In the truck, a hidden compartment. No one'll find it, but it's accessible.'

'Be careful, Mike. I've got a bad feeling about this. Not about Rose, about the whole situation. There's a woman involved, a woman you care about way too much for common sense, and that could throw you off, make you do something stupid. I don't want you hurt.' She reached up and kissed him on the lips, a cool, dry kiss between dear friends.

Ramsey hugged her, holding her blond head against his heart for a brief moment before letting her go. 'It's too late for that, Kat,' he said. 'Way too late for that.'

8

Saturday evening, Salt Lake City

Ramsey zipped his sports bag shut and dialed the number for the room next door. Kathleen answered on the first ring. 'Rose'll be ready to leave in ten minutes,' he said, checking his watch. Eight o'clock already, a little later than he'd planned. He hoped Rose had slept better than he had. He'd tossed and turned throughout the day, not falling asleep until late afternoon.

Probably had something to do with that twelve hour marathon sleep he'd had the previous day. That and the fact Rose hadn't offered another back rub.

'We'll grab a bite to eat, then head out. Give me at least fifteen minutes before you follow. I do not want to see you in my rearview mirror, understood? Don't argue, Kat . . . Thank you,' he said, laughing, 'but I don't think that's anatomically possible. Did she make any calls? Just the one to me, *hmmm*? Okay. Remember to stay back. Headlights show up for miles on the salt flats and I don't want anyone to know you're

141

there. Only in your dreams, darlin'. Thanks, I'll be careful.'

Ramsey slowly replaced the phone. Kathleen worried too much. Nothing implicated Rose so far, there was no reason to suspect the hijackers would strike. This trip was going to be a complete waste.

Except for meeting Rose. Ramsey choked down the bitter regret over what could never be. Damn, it was going to be a long drive to California. If nothing happened, he'd just have to run it again and again until the gang was stopped.

Trip after lonely trip across the country, without Rose. He'd grown used to having her beside him in the cab of the big diesel. Hell, he'd grown used to having her near, no matter where.

He grabbed his bag and left the room, closing the door behind him. The air was clear, the evening cold and growing dark.

An older compact car with 'just married' painted along the side and balloons tied to the radio antennae pulled into the space near Rose's room. A young man and woman got out, laughing, shaking something out of their clothing.

Birdseed. Ramsey smiled, watching them brush the seeds out of their hair, empty it from their shoes. They kissed through their laughter. Would he ever feel that carefree, ever share such a scene with a woman?

With Rose. Ramsey shivered, more from a sense of foreboding than the chill air, and turned away from the couple's passionate embrace. He looked directly into Rose's wary eyes.

'Are you ready to go?' she asked. Her parka hung open, revealing a bright yellow tee-shirt tucked into her Wranglers, but Rose's dark green eyes looked empty. The deep shadows beneath them told him she hadn't slept any better than he had.

'Yeah. Let's stash our bags in the truck, then grab dinner.' He picked up the small pile of luggage near the door and turned to leave. 'Do you want to call your aunt before we go?' he asked.

'I already did,' Rose answered, leading the way out of the room. 'I talked to her earlier today. I was right. She did go out and play poker last night. I told her not to expect us until Monday. I don't want her to worry.'

Kathleen said Rose hadn't called anyone. How could Kathleen have missed the call to her aunt? What else might his partner have missed? Frowning, Ramsey followed Rose out to the truck, carrying the bags. 'Why don't you go on ahead.' He nodded in the direction of the diner just across the street. 'It'll take less time if you order for me. I need to check the tie-downs and make sure all my paperwork is in order.'

And ask Kathleen about that call.

'What should I order for you? My taste buds are clamoring for a greasy hamburger.' Her words might be teasing, but Ramsey detected the edge of hurt in her voice. Guilt washed over him in waves. He wanted Rose back, exactly as she'd been before he pushed her away.

'Have your taste buds discussed it with your arteries? That place looks like it specializes in grease.' His retort sounded light, but felt awkward. He missed the easy banter they'd shared earlier.

He tossed the bags into the cab. When he turned around, he saw her shoulders rise and fall with a deep sigh. When she straightened her spine and faced him, Ramsey sensed she had come to a momentous decision. Was she thinking of going on without him? He clenched his fists, waiting, but she simply asked, 'What should I order for you?'

'Burger and fries.' He wondered if somehow he'd missed another subtle change in their relationship. She certainly kept him off balance. 'And coffee. Lots of coffee.'

'Antacids on the side?' She smiled at him. This time, a smile that reached her eyes and lit them with green fire. Ramsey's heart did a complete flip. Was it really all that important he figure her out?

'Main course,' he quipped and she laughed at his stupid joke, then turned and headed across the street. He watched until she was safely inside the small restaurant before going in search of Kathleen.

It didn't take him long to find her. She waited behind the truck, within hearing of his conversation with Rose. She'd obviously been eavesdropping.

'Enjoy your snooping?' he asked. *What a childish thing to say* . . . Kathleen was only doing her job, much better, in fact, than he was.

'Actually, yes.' Kathleen grinned at him. 'I can't believe she laughs at your dorky jokes. It must be love. And by the way, I had my window open and heard what she said about calling her aunt. There's no way, Ramsey. The only call she made was to you. Any reason why she'd lie?'

'Hell, I'm beginning to wonder if this marvelous aunt of hers even exists. Rose claimed to be talking to her yesterday morning, but when she handed me the phone all I heard was dead air.'

Kathleen's smile was absolutely huge. 'I think you've answered my question. She probably invented Aunt Rosa for protection.'

'Protection! From what?' Ramsey demanded. 'And wipe that smirk off your face.'

'From you, Lothario. She wants you to think there's someone expecting to hear from her on a regular basis. She didn't know you from a hole in the wall when she accepted your offer of a ride. Aunt Rosa's her chaperone. It makes perfectly good sense.'

'Well, you don't,' Ramsey grumbled.

'Only because you're a man, and a little thick between the ears. Go for it, Ramsey. She loves you, you love her. You get so disgustingly gooey-eyed every time you mention her name it makes me wanna puke. That's got to mean something.'

'Only that you've got a weak stomach, Malone.' Ramsey reached out to tweak her under the chin, only to pull his hand back when Kathleen's expression suddenly turned serious.

'I'm not kidding, Mike. Sometimes it only happens once in a lifetime. Don't blow your chance. I've got a good feeling about her. She's okay. If she loves you as much as I think she does, you'll work out the small stuff.'

'Suspecting her of theft is small stuff?' He made no attempt to mask his sarcasm.

'Yeah. If you love each other it is. Good luck. I'll follow you to Sacramento and we'll plan the next run. I bet we'll have to schedule it around your wedding.'

★ ★ ★

For once, Rose was tempted to disagree with her aunt's advice. She'd been ready to either rent a car in Salt Lake City or catch a plane and continue on to California alone. Knowing how Ramsey felt and as confused as she was about her own feelings, Rose wasn't sure she could survive the next couple of days traveling with him.

But Aunt Rosa had been adamant. It was too dangerous to drive alone and she didn't want to worry about Rose flying with all the crazy weather they'd had. Her arguments didn't make a lick of sense to Rose, but it was so rare her aunt asked anything of her, Rose had finally agreed to continue the trip with Ramsey.

She'd tried to explain to her aunt that matchmaking was a waste of time. Aunt Rosa had laughed, implying Rose didn't know what she was talking about. When Rose repeated Ramsey's comments about not ever settling down, Aunt Rosa had laughed even harder, and in her deep gravely voice said, 'Methinks he doth protest too much, and so doth *you*.'

So much for the calm voice of reason Rose

had hoped to hear.

The restaurant was almost full and noisy in the usual way of any all-night diner located near a busy highway interchange. Rose spotted an empty booth near the back, away from other patrons. Within moments, a gum-snapping, middle-aged waitress with brick red hair had taken Rose's order and filled both coffee cups.

Rose wondered idly if truck stops across the country had a mandatory dress code. Short polyester skirts, frilly aprons and sensible shoes appeared to be the national uniform.

She glanced out the window in time to see Ramsey walking across the street toward her. He had his hands stuffed in his pockets, his head was bowed, and he looked as if the weight of the world rested on his shoulders.

She wondered how much of that weight she'd caused.

Ramsey slid into the booth across from her. He looked exhausted.

'Are you okay?' she asked.

'Yeah. Didn't sleep worth a damn.' He took a swallow of his coffee and stared into the steam rising from the cup.

Rose noticed where he'd nicked himself shaving, a tiny red crease beneath his chin. 'Looks like you tried to cut your throat tonight,' she said, trying to make him smile.

'You offering to finish the job?'

'They say the only way to get a job done right is to send a woman.' Rose took a small sip of the strong coffee.

'I doubt that applies to shaving.'

'I was talking about cutting your throat. But, if we're talking about shaving, I've got you beat there, too. Consider the percentage.'

'Excuse me?'

'Percentage, Ramsey. The percentage of body area shaved. I think I've got you beat.' She stretched her denim-clad legs out in front of him, gratified when he swallowed deeply and looked away. At least he wasn't oblivious to her. She felt perversely sorry it was too cold out to wear shorts. Knowing Ramsey suffered as much as she did had a definite appeal.

* * *

They may have been covered in serviceable blue denim, but when Rose extended those long legs in front of him, Ramsey saw smooth skin that went on forever. He couldn't shake the vision burned into his brain of Rose wrapped in a skimpy little bath towel.

And she had absolutely no idea what she did to him.

149

Ramsey gritted his teeth, relieved when the waitress slapped two huge hamburgers and a big basket of fries down on the table between them. Rose carefully spread gobs of mustard, catsup and mayonnaise on both sides of her bun, then smooshed the sandwich together to get it into her mouth.

'If this doesn't kill us, nothing will,' Ramsey said, biting into a crispy French fry. 'There can't be any nutritional value in a meal like this.'

'Of course there is.' Rose wiped a glob of mustard off her chin. 'All the food groups are here.' She pulled the top of the bun to one side, then had to slide the lettuce and tomato and pickles back on the meat patty. 'Veggies, meat, cheese, grains . . . '

'Grease.'

'That's the most important one of all.' She laughed, reassembled her burger and took another big bite.

Kathleen was right, Ramsey thought. When he looked at Rose, he could see himself with a family, a future. He chewed thoughtfully on his hamburger, thinking of his partner's advice. *Go for it*, she'd said. Kathleen's instincts were as good as Ramsey's.

Right now they were probably better. She didn't have hormones messing up her concentration.

If Kathleen thought Rose was innocent, Ramsey was inclined to agree. A little loony, maybe, if she'd invented Aunt Rosa as protection. If he were to invent a guardian angel, it'd be someone with a black belt in karate, not a seventy-five year old lady with a penchant for poker.

But there were so many stumbling blocks to get through, so many questions to answer, so . . . The curious expression on Rose's face dragged Ramsey back to the present. She stared beyond him, past his shoulder as if she recognized someone. A tiny frown puckered between her dark brows.

Ramsey twisted slowly in his seat to see what had caught her attention. Two men stood at the cash register, both nondescript, dressed in jeans and heavy flannel shirts. One wore a western hat and a heavy sheepskin coat with the collar rolled up, the other had on a soiled ball cap and a dark blue down vest.

The one in the vest picked up his change and they both left the diner. Ramsey turned back to Rose, intrigued by her perplexed expression.

'Anyone you know?' he asked.

'I'm not sure. I could've sworn the one in the sheepskin coat was James's old fraternity brother from college, but Tim's supposed to

151

be vacationing in Bermuda right now.' She shrugged her shoulders. 'I must've been mistaken.'

'Did you recognize the other guy?'

'No. I wasn't really paying attention to him.'

Ramsey mentally filed the incident away. Hadn't Tim Anderson been the hijackers' first victim? He'd contact Kathleen, have her check on the two men. Hiding his concerns, he grinned at Rose. 'You weren't paying attention because you had food in front of you,' he teased.

'Gonna make something of it, Ramsey?' She waved a French fry under his nose. 'You think I'm getting fat?'

'I never said a word.'

He leaned over and bit the fry off, nipping the tips of Rose's fingers. She laughed and pulled her hand back.

'And you won't, if you know what's good for you.'

'That's my problem, Rose.' Ramsey grabbed another fry. 'I haven't figured out what's good for me.'

★ ★ ★

'You weren't kidding about the antacids,' Rose muttered awhile later over the low rumble of the diesel engine. 'What's the matter? Hamburger fighting back?' Ramsey laughed, then failed to suppress a grumbly belch.

'I rest my case.' Rose reached for her purse. 'If I'm lucky there may still be a few left in here.'

'Is there anything you don't carry in that bag?' Ramsey winked at Rose, then scanned the dark horizon. The salt flats stretched for endless miles, glowing faintly in the pale gleam of a quarter moon. He wondered if Kathleen had had any luck checking on Tim Anderson. Ramsey'd contacted his partner from the diner while Rose went to the restroom.

'I've got some!' Grinning triumphantly, Rose held a small roll in her hand. 'Now we deal,' she said. 'What will you give me for two Rolaids? Bids are starting at five dollars apiece.'

'Bids are starting at me not leaving you on the side of the road with your thumb in the air.' Ramsey reached for the packet.

'Spoilsport,' Rose grumbled, grabbing two of the white tablets for herself before handing the pack to Ramsey.

Their fingers barely touched, merely a whisper of contact. Ramsey felt it all the way to his toes. Shaken, he fumbled with the tight wrapper until Rose took the packet from him, removed two of the tablets and dropped them into his outstretched hand. Without a word, she scrunched back against the door.

Kathleen was right. Only a fool would deny this.

He looked to his right, directly into Rose's deep green eyes.

She watched him, both hands clasped tightly in her lap.

Ramsey knew she'd felt the same shock, the same sense of destiny that had followed them every day since he'd rescued her.

He dragged his gaze away from Rose, thankful for the lack of traffic, the arrow-straight road, the wide empty lanes. It was a good thing this sense of the inevitable hadn't swamped him while he crossed the Rockies, or he'd have wrecked the truck.

At least they hadn't been hijacked. Kathleen was right. Rose must be innocent. The hijackers looking for this load were in the wrong place, because Rose hadn't given him away.

She hadn't given him away because she wasn't involved.

Ramsey took a deep breath. He wondered if the time would ever be right to take a chance, to tell Rose how he felt. To tell her she'd managed to breach his defenses.

Was the time ever right to tell a woman she was not only the object of his greatest desire, she was also the object of his criminal investigation?

That she would continue as a suspect, no matter how innocent he might believe her to be, until the case was solved?

Damn.

He glanced once again at the pale quarter moon, surprised to see it hanging blood-red in the night sky.

Red? 'What, the . . . ? Rose! Do you see any lights nearby, any sign of buildings?' He scanned the horizon, dismayed by the sudden darkness where moonlight had once glistened on the desert. *Damn!* Why hadn't he paid more attention to the weather reports and less to the woman sitting beside him?

'What's the matter?' Panic edged Rose's words. She had no idea.

'Sandstorm,' he said between clenched teeth. He didn't need this. Ramsey down-shifted and took a sharp turn off the highway, onto a rutted country road. 'It'll take the paint right off this scraper, not to mention the new chrome on Handy's truck. I think I see a barn up ahead. Maybe we can pull inside out of the wind, or at least park behind the thing.'

The massive barn appeared to be the remnant of an old homestead. One large door tilted at a crazy angle and cast weird shadows in the strong beam from the truck's headlights. Ramsey braked, threw the gears into neutral and opened the cab door. The howling wind almost ripped it out of his grasp.

Jumping to the ground, he forced the door shut behind him to protect Rose, then ran through the stinging grains of sand until he reached the barn. Squinting through narrowed lids, he struggled with the ancient wooden doors, finally sliding one side along rusted rollers until he had an opening barely large enough for the huge truck and scraper.

Within moments, he'd climbed back into the diesel and moved the truck and its load inside the relative safety of the barn. After a brief struggle, he managed to close the heavy door behind them.

'Rose . . . over here!' He gestured in the direction of a large stack of baled hay piled haphazardly against one end of the building. 'We need to move those hay bales against the wall. That wind's gonna get a lot stronger before the storm's over.'

Rose quickly climbed down out of the cab. The headlights from the diesel illuminated the vast interior of the dilapidated structure. The entire building shook with the force of the wind. She shivered, more from fear than

156

cold, frightened by the swirling dust blowing unabated through wide cracks on the windward side of the building.

She reached Ramsey's side and grabbed the wire wrapped around one end of a bale of hay. 'This stuff's heavier than it looks!' she shouted, alarmed by the keening howl of the storm. Loose boards on the upper half of the barn banged and creaked in the wind, threatening to break free. Sand sliced between warped and missing boards, stinging unprotected skin.

'No kidding.' Ramsey grunted as he tugged yet another bale against the ramshackle wall, adding support against the force of the storm.

They worked in silence after that, frantically hauling bale after ancient bale of hay to build a strong barrier between the cutting sand and the shiny, chrome covered truck with its valuable cargo.

Rose finally slumped against the closed door of the cab and drew a deep, ragged breath. She'd worked steadily beside Ramsey for over an hour, reinforcing the wall, protecting the equipment from the frightening storm raging outside.

A storm that couldn't even compare to the raging emotions swirling inside her. She watched Ramsey as he checked the stability of the wall they'd built. Working by his side had raised her awareness of him to an even greater level. His muscles bunching as he lifted the heavy bales, the look of raw determination each time he glanced in her direction.

What was he thinking? Was he wondering about the strange chemistry that linked them, or just worrying about his damned truck? *Probably the truck.* She grinned in spite of herself, bent at the waist and finger-combed her hair, trying to shake the sand and hay out of it.

What a mess! She wiped grit from the corners of her mouth. Sand was everywhere. She checked her pockets, searching for a stick of gum to clear the dust out of her mouth. All she could find was the tiny pack of antacids. She popped the last one in her mouth and pretended it was a mint.

When Rose glanced up, she looked directly into Ramsey's gray eyes. Her own eyes widened in response. He watched her, staring with an intensity that linked them in an almost physical sense. It could have been frightening, to be the object of such intense study. Instead, Rose knew a sudden sense of calm, a feeling that all was as it should be and she had nothing to fear from Michael Ramsey.

Nothing but herself.

'Do I frighten you, Rose?' he asked, his voice a soft rumble out of the darkness.

As if he reads my mind. She stilled, suddenly aware of her heart beating, her blood rushing through her veins. Waited, wondering at the expression clouding Ramsey's gray eyes.

'I hope I do, you know, because you scare the hell out of me.'

'I don't understand.' Why did he keep doing this to her, throwing her off balance, asking her questions without answers? Rose moistened her lips, fighting the need to clear her throat. The antacid had left a flavor of minty chalk in her mouth. It might as well have been sand.

'I'm not very good at this, I guess. Talking to a woman. I — ' He stepped closer, then reached up and pulled a piece of straw out of her hair.

'What's going on, Ramsey?' she demanded, masking her confusion. The storm howled unabated, adding an eerie sense of unreality to the scene. Ramsey stepped back, dropped his hands to his sides and sighed heavily.

'A friend of mine told me we sometimes get just one chance at love.' He reached out again to touch Rose's hair. She felt his fingers caress the loose strands around her face and fought the need to press her cheek against his

159

hand. 'My friend said if we miss that chance, it might never happen again. Rose, I've been fighting what I feel for you since the moment you awakened in my arms. It's been eating me up inside . . . '

'It's okay,' she whispered, turning to catch his long fingers between her lips for a brief kiss. 'I understand what you're trying to say. You're afraid you might be falling for me and you don't want to. It's okay, really. I understand.' She turned away from his touch, proud of the thin veneer of control she'd managed to hang onto.

'Dammit, quit puttin' words in my mouth, Rose! That's not what I was trying to say at all!'

'Oh?'

'I was trying to say that I'm through fighting it, that I'm tired of all the word games . . . and that I care about you. And I think you care about me, only you're too pigheaded to admit it.'

'No, I'm not!' Sputtering, Rose backed away. 'I don't know how I feel about you. That's the truth, Ramsey. I'm confused. I've never felt this way about anyone, not even the man I was planning to marry. It scares me.'

'It doesn't have to.'

She felt the rough surface of his palm against her cheek, the featherlight whisper of

160

his lips as he spoke the words into the heavy fall of her hair. 'Not if we're in this together, Rose. From the way things sound to me, we're definitely in agreement.'

'It'll be the first time we've ever agreed on anything,' Rose muttered, unwilling to let go of her anger quite so easily. She was definitely not pigheaded! Nor did she ask confusing questions, or switch from hot to cold in a heartbeat.

'I hope it's not the last time.' Ramsey whispered against her lips, parting them easily with the lightest touch of his tongue. 'God, you taste good,' he growled, delving deeper into her mouth. His hands tangled in the heavy fall of hair at the back of her neck.

Rose pulled away, her laughter bubbling just below the surface. 'I taste like Rolaids, Ramsey,' she said dryly, fighting the heat that drained her limbs of their strength.

'Only you would get indigestion from my kisses,' he muttered, pulling Rose once again into his embrace. 'I don't know why I even try.'

'Because you can't help yourself?' Rose grabbed Ramsey by the front of his shirt and kissed him, parting his mouth, tasting with lips and teeth and tongue as if to devour him.

He pressed her back against the side of the cab and she felt his hand slip into the tight waistband of her jeans. He pulled the cotton tee-shirt loose and placed his cool palm against the smooth flesh of her belly.

Rose gasped, the sensation of his touch spreading like liquid fire until she thought her knees might buckle. The kiss she had started had suddenly become Ramsey's, his lips taking, his tongue tasting. His fingers traveled along the line of her ribs until she wanted to die with the pleasure.

His fingertips found the pebbly surface of her nipple and teased her through the light silk of her bra and still his mouth plundered hers. All she could do was hang on to his shoulders and pray that Ramsey was strong enough to hold the two of them upright.

His kiss shattered her defenses, drawing a reaction from Rose unlike any she'd experienced, drawing her farther and farther away from the unanswered questions, the unfamiliar fears.

A small part of her mind knew they had to stop, had to draw this wonderful torture to a close before they went too far, took too many chances with emotions too fresh and uncertain.

Ramsey'd talked about love, but he hadn't said he loved her. He didn't need to. His kisses told Rose everything she wanted to know. She smiled against his lips, then pulled her mouth gently away from his. Resting her forehead against Ramsey's solid chest, she drew in deep gulps of air.

'I think the storm's finally dying down,' she said. Ramsey chuckled, and his laughter echoed against her ear.

'Which storm?' he asked, brushing the damp strands of hair back from her heated face. 'Mine's still raging, thanks to you.'

'I'm sorry, I — '

'Don't be. This isn't the place or the time. But if you don't mind, I think I'll just go outside and check the weather.'

'Are you sure it's safe?'

'A lot safer than it is in here,' he teased, kissing her gently along her hairline, even nibbling the edge of her ear.

Rose shivered. 'Then go,' she ordered, giggling at his tender kisses. This was a side of Ramsey she hadn't expected, light and tender, playful.

He went. She watched him slide the heavy door to one side and disappear into the silent darkness. The storm had ended as quickly as it had begun.

Rose's lips tingled, her heart still thudded uncontrollably in her chest and Ramsey's taste lingered in her senses. She leaned against the cab to ponder the maelstrom of sensations, when suddenly, something clattered at the far end of the barn, beyond the beam from the truck's headlights.

'Ramsey? Is that you?' He must be trying to come in through another door. Rose picked her way carefully across the littered floor. She headed for a small doorway at the back of the barn.

'I'm coming.' She stepped carefully over old tractor parts and pieces of ancient farm equipment, then collided with the edge of a metal trailer. 'Ouch,' she muttered, rubbing her bruised shin. Why couldn't he just come back in the way he'd left?

A sudden movement caught her attention. Rose whirled. Her scream caught in her throat as a huge man, dark and menacing, loomed up out of the shadows and towered over her.

Rose screamed, backed away in terror, then screamed again as something caught her ankles, wrapped about her legs, then toppled her to the ground at the stranger's feet.

9

Saturday night, Utah Desert

'They wouldn't tell you anything? Damn. Well, do your best to catch up. I'll take my time getting us back on the road. Bye, Kat.'

Ramsey slipped the cell phone back into his pocket and stared out across the moonlit desert. The storm had blown through, leaving only silence and sand drifts in its wake.

Tim Anderson had reservations at a very nice hotel in St. George, in the Bermuda Islands, right where Rose said he should be. Unfortunately, the hotel staff's unwillingness to confirm if he'd actually checked in had stopped Kathleen's investigation cold.

Maybe Rose only imagined seeing Tim Anderson at the diner, maybe she'd brought his name up to throw Ramsey off her track.

Maybe she'd practically made love to him a little while ago as a way to take his mind off the investigation. She'd been the one in control, the one who pulled away at the last possible moment. Control'd been the last thing on Ramsey's mind.

She was either innocent or guilty. He had

to assume one and stick with it, or go nuts thinking about it. 'Maybe it's too late, maybe I'm already crazy,' he muttered. Okay, decision time. He'd assume she was innocent.

And if you're wrong? his conscience asked.

'If I'm wrong, and we're hijacked, I've got no partner for back-up because Kat's at least an hour east of here.' *Good Lord*, he thought, chagrined. *I'm talking to myself. Definitely not a good sign.*

Neither he nor Kathleen had expected her investigation into Anderson's whereabouts to take so long, or prove so fruitless.

Could anything else possibly go wrong?

Sighing deeply, Ramsey turned and slipped back into the barn.

Rose's scream echoed through the huge building.

His reaction was pure reflex powered by surging adrenaline. Ramsey raced to the truck, grabbed the door of the cab and slipped his .38 Police Special out of its hiding place. Then he slid quietly down the side of the truck, hiding himself in the dark shadows out of the glare of the headlights. A muffled thump sounded from the far end of the barn.

The indistinguishable mutter of voices.

Ramsey held the revolver steady in his right hand, moving with guarded stealth in the direction of the noise. Another sound, a strangled, angry moan, made his heart race. He forced himself to proceed slowly, carefully.

Something moved, a shadow within a shadow hidden from Ramsey's view by the rusting carcass of an ancient tractor. He stopped, motionless, not even daring to draw a breath.

'No! Don't!'

Rose! Ramsey held the gun in both hands, took a deep breath and swung around the end of the tractor.

The cell phone in his pocket beeped.

Somewhere overhead an owl hooted.

Rose, sprawled on the floor, gaped at Ramsey and screamed again.

And a gray-haired gentleman in coveralls took one look at the ugly revolver pointed at his face and quietly passed out at Ramsey's feet.

'Are you all right?'

Ramsey knelt in front of Rose, but all she saw was the gun he kept trained on the stranger. The cell phone beeped again.

Ramsey reached into his pocket and shut the phone off with his free hand, still holding the revolver steady on the prostrate form of the old man.

Why would a truck driver carry a gun? Not only carry it, but handle it as naturally as if it were an extension of his arm?

'Rose? What happened? Who's this guy?' Ramsey nudged the old man's limp body with the barrel of his revolver.

The man's mouth opened in a deep, reverberating snore that ended in a long whistle.

'Get that thing away from him.' She gestured at the revolver. 'He startled me and I tripped. I think he's drunk. He didn't hurt me. He was just trying to help me up.' She glared at the revolver Ramsey still aimed in the general direction of the old man. 'Why do you have a gun?' she demanded.

'I heard you scream. I figured you were in trouble.'

'That doesn't answer my question. Where did you get the gun?' Rose struggled to untangle her feet from the pile of rope she'd stumbled into when the stranger startled her.

Ramsey didn't answer. He merely slipped the revolver into the deep inner pocket of his leather jacket, casually, as if he'd done the same thing hundreds of times before. Then he leaned over and put his ear against the old man's chest.

'Is he okay?' Rose asked, tugging the boot off her trapped foot, then pulling the twisted rope over the ends of her toes. Obviously Ramsey didn't want to talk about the gun.

She shuddered, reminded once again of how very little she knew about him.

They'd almost made love, right here in this ramshackle barn with a drunken old man as witness. Rose flushed hot and cold at the same time, remembering the heat from Ramsey's kisses, the gentle caress of his roughened fingers stroking her breasts.

He'd said this was neither the time nor the place. Talk about an understatement!

Another loud snore bubbled out between the old man's slack lips. Ramsey jerked quickly away and sat back on his heels. 'Phew. You're right, he's drunk. Where'd he come from? I heard you scream. You're okay?'

'I'm fine. He just scared me half to death.' She retied her boot and stood up, brushing straw and dust from her jeans. She realized her hands were trembling.

'I'll take care of our guest.'

'You do that.' Rose noticed how quickly Ramsey averted his eyes from her direct gaze. *He's hiding something*, she thought. The image of the axe murderer returned, except this time it didn't seem so comical.

Instead of an axe, he'd been holding a very lethal-looking revolver. Holding it as naturally as he held a phone.

Rose turned and walked stiffly back to the truck. She climbed into the cab and tried to force the image of Ramsey grasping the revolver out of her mind, but her thoughts still scattered in a thousand directions.

Maybe Ramsey carried a gun because of the hijackings, maybe all of Handy Hannibal's drivers carried weapons. She wasn't so naive to think concealed weapon laws had much of an effect on an individual bound and determined to arm himself, especially with the current rash of thefts and assaults.

On the other hand, she'd accepted Ramsey's story that he worked for Handy Hannibal without ever checking it out with the little man. What if Ramsey had lied? He could be a member of the hijackers' ring. Instead of delivering a legal shipment across country, what if he were moving a piece of stolen equipment? That would explain his desire to drive only at night, to take a different route than the one agreed upon.

It would explain the gun.

But it wouldn't explain Mike Ramsey. Not his kindness to everyone they'd met on this odd journey, nor his heroic rescue of Rose.

Or the way Rose felt about him, this unsettling mix of wonderment laced with fear. There could be only one explanation.

This must be love, this painful, exhilarating feeling lifting her up and turning her inside out.

Confusing her senses, upending her organized, logical world.

'Are you okay?'

Startled, Rose swung around to her right. Ramsey peered in through the open cab window.

'I'm sorry. I didn't mean to startle you. I just wanted you to know your buddy was going to be all right.' He nodded toward the back of the barn.

'Who is he? He scared me half to death, looming up out of the darkness like that.'

'A transient, I guess, although it's pretty isolated out here for a homeless person. There's a little makeshift living area back there and what looks like an old still.'

'A still? Like for making whiskey? You're kidding. I didn't even notice it.'

'Hasn't been used for years, from the looks of things, but there're enough old bottles of moonshine to last someone a mighty long time.' He chuckled, nodding again in the old man's direction. 'He probably stumbled in here one day and thought he'd found heaven. I stuck him back in his bedroll to sleep it off. We can stop at the next town and notify authorities, make sure someone checks up on him. In the meantime, when he wakes up we'll be gone, and he'll think he had one heck of a dream.'

171

'More like a nightmare.' Rose glanced away from Ramsey.

'No, Rose. A dream . . . you were in it.'

Rose turned slowly and gazed back at Ramsey. She saw herself reflected in the dark pools beneath his lashes. Her own eyes filled with unshed tears. Love couldn't possibly exist without trust, trust was impossible without honesty. 'A nightmare, Ramsey,' she answered reluctantly. 'Dreams don't have guns in them.'

The silence lay thick and heavy between them.

'I guess they don't,' Ramsey said. He watched her for a long, silent moment. 'You know, we live in dangerous times.' His eyes darkened, he shrugged his shoulders, stepped down off the running board and started to walk away. 'I'll get the door,' he said. 'We need to be going.'

The flat, lifeless quality of his voice wasn't lost on Rose. She answered in the same tone. 'Do all of Handy's drivers carry weapons?' she asked.

Ramsey didn't turn around. His shoulders sagged, then straightened. 'No,' he said, after a long pause. 'Handy's drivers don't carry guns.'

She waited for an explanation. The silence stretched between them with no sign of closure. Rose shut her eyes and drew a great breath against the pain as it slowly tightened like a band about her chest.

'I'm ready to leave when you are,' she said, speaking to his broad back. He merely grunted in acknowledgment. 'By the way,' she asked, determined to get a response out of him, 'Did you ever figure out who called earlier? I thought I heard the cell phone.'

Ramsey shrugged his shoulders, then turned his head, looked over his shoulder and grinned at Rose as if the uncomfortable exchange had never passed between them.

He's doing it again, dammit. How could she possibly understand his easy shift of temperament, his ability to mask his emotions?

Would she ever really know Mike Ramsey?

'I'm surprised you could hear it and scream at the same time,' he said. 'You scared me half to death, you know.'

'I'm so sorry,' she answered sarcastically, falling much too easily back into their typical banter. 'I don't enjoy singular terror. It's much more rewarding as a group activity.'

'I guess that makes sense, in some convoluted, female fashion. You're certainly giving me enough damsel-rescuing practice. How often do you intend for me to pull your tush out of the fire, literally and figuratively speaking, before this trip ends?'

Ramsey's dry question brought a reluctant smile to Rose's lips. 'Tired of playing Ramsey to the rescue?' she asked. *He should be*, she thought, suddenly embarrassed. He hadn't known she wasn't in any real danger, yet he'd still rushed to her defense. She hadn't thanked him, hadn't done anything but wonder about the damned gun. She still wondered. He hadn't given her much of an answer.

'Never.' He flashed a broad grin. 'Makes me feel real macho.'

'Like you need to feel more macho. Or is that what the gun's for?' she asked, cringing inwardly at the disparaging sound in her voice. Why wouldn't he tell her? What was he hiding?

Once again the smile left Ramsey's face. 'Like I told you before Rose, we live in dangerous times.' He studied her a moment in silence. 'I checked the call return on the cell phone,' he added. 'It was my boss. He'd been trying to reach me for a couple of hours. I've already called him back, and told him everything's okay, that we'd be in Sacramento Monday morning.'

We live in dangerous times. That was an understatement. Was Ramsey part of that danger? Torn, Rose struggled for a calm, conversational tone. 'I thought maybe my aunt might've tried to call.'

'In the middle of the night?' He tilted his head and looked up at her, a curious expression on his face. 'Why would she call? You told me you already talked to her today.'

'I don't know . . . I guess it's just that Aunt Rosa always seems to sense when I need her,' she finished lamely.

'And you need her tonight?' Ramsey stepped back up on the running board, bringing himself to eye level with Rose.

She met his direct gaze with her own. 'I thought I did. Earlier.' Why was it suddenly difficult to breathe? She felt trapped, a willing victim, but trapped nonetheless, by his dark eyes.

'How much earlier, Rose? When you helped me stack the hay bales against the storm? Or maybe when we kissed?' He leaned in through the open window and touched her lips lightly with his, then backed away. 'Does that threaten you, Rose? Do I threaten you?'

'I don't know, Ramsey,' she answered honestly. 'Sometimes I think I know you, then I realize I haven't figured you out at all. I do know you scare the hell out of me.'

'Good.' Grinning broadly, he leaned over and kissed her lightly on the tip of the nose. 'That's what I wanted to hear. Now let's get going.'

* ★ ★ ★

'We're about four hours from Elko,' Ramsey
said as he guided the big rig back onto the
highway. 'I know it's been a long night, but if
you can handle it, I'd like to drive straight
through. We can be there by about seven a.m.
We'll grab a bite to eat, a few hours sleep,
then we should be able to make it into
Sacramento by Monday morning.'

'*Long night?*' *That's an understatement.*
Rose watched Ramsey's strong hands grip the
heavy steering wheel. This had been one of
the longest nights of her life and it wasn't
close to ending. 'You're the driver.' She
shrugged her shoulders. 'The point is, can
you handle it?'

'I can handle anything, sweetheart. Anything at all,' Ramsey growled in a deep, sexy
voice.

'Guess I left myself wide open for that one,'
Rose admitted dryly, laughing in spite of
herself. 'What I meant to say was . . . '

'Don't worry.' He reached across the cab
and touched her lightly on the shoulder.
'We'll stop in Wendover for coffee and a
break. I'd never put you in danger. I know
enough not to drive when I'm too tired.'

'Thanks.' What more could she say? This
wasn't the time to bring up all her

unanswered questions. He probably wouldn't answer them anyway.

She knew the gun wasn't in his pocket anymore. He'd left his coat lying across the seat. Uncomfortable as it made her feel to go through his belongings, Rose had searched the coat while Ramsey was busy checking the tie-downs on the load.

She had no idea where he'd hidden the damned thing. Or when. She hated spying on Ramsey, resented the guilt she felt over going through his pockets. At the same time, she wished he'd leave his wallet lying around long enough for her to get a look at his identification.

No matter how much she wanted to trust him or how much she might think she loved him, Rose needed answers. *You'll have to trust me*, he'd said. Had Ramsey been thinking of a situation like this when he'd instigated that odd conversation with Rose?

For all his good points, Mike Ramsey obviously considered his secrets more important than their fragile relationship. Sighing, Rose settled back against the warm leather. Maybe once they got to California she'd be able to figure out what in the heck was going on.

Ramsey glanced in Rose's direction, then turned his attention back to the long ribbon of highway stretching out before him. Thank goodness she finally slept. At least then she couldn't ask him about the damned revolver.

Definitely a stupid move on his part, charging in with his gun drawn to rescue the damsel in distress. Except she hadn't been in all that much distress. Not so much that she hadn't been more interested in his firearm than the old coot who'd frightened her in the first place.

No, this damsel was too smart and much too tenacious to let the matter drop. Handy's drivers never carried guns. They'd be fired without compunction if they tried to get away with a concealed firearm on one of Handy's rigs. Ramsey didn't want to get the old man in trouble by letting Rose think it was an accepted practice.

He'd have to invent another reason, fast, before she got nosy enough to actually check up on him. Then again, maybe she'd just accept that obtuse, *we live in dangerous times*, comment. Right, he thought. *Oh, what a tangled web we weave* . . .

But they did live in dangerous times. Very dangerous.

And he still had absolutely no idea if Rose was guilty or innocent.

The cell phone beeped. Rose stirred, then settled back to sleep. Quickly Ramsey picked up the phone before the tone sounded a second time.

'Ramsey here . . . yeah, we're almost to Wendover.' He glanced again in Rose's direction. She slept soundly, her eyes tightly closed, a small frown creasing the space between her brows. Kat asked him his plans. 'I plan to stop there for a break, give you time to catch up, then head on to Elko before we get a room . . . I figure about five and a half, six hours to Reno, then it's a straight shot down to Sacramento . . . another one? . . . damn. Yeah, that country around Yerington's pretty desolate . . . I'll get back to you . . . bye, Kat.'

Ramsey replaced the cell phone in its holder, then checked the rearview mirror. Kathleen was still a good forty-five miles back, too far to help if he needed her. She'd better catch up in Wendover.

Ramsey's sense of unease had grown steadily. He wanted his partner close by. She'd been in touch with headquarters. There'd been another hijacking just a few hours ago, about twenty-five miles west of Lovelock. The thieves were obviously working this area, had practically shut down their operations on the east coast.

Why here? Why not the more heavily traveled southern route? Coincidence? Ramsey clenched his teeth, unable to accept the odds, unwilling to believe a case growing stronger against Rose each day.

Kathleen said the victim was another Acme Insurance client. One of Rose's.

He glanced in her direction. She slept the sleep of the innocent, her hair falling in dark waves across her cheek, spilling over her full breasts, pooling like liquid silk in her lap.

Ramsey's breath caught in his throat. Even with all his suspicions, with the tiny bits and pieces of circumstantial evidence growing against her, he wanted Rose. Even more frightening, he needed her.

The lights of a small restaurant lit up the sky ahead. Ramsey downshifted and guided the huge rig into the parking lot. Rose stirred beside him, then straightened up, rubbing her eyes.

'Where are we?' she asked, her voice heavy with sleep.

'Wendover. I need some coffee, a sandwich, maybe. How about you?'

'I guess I could eat something.'

Ramsey parked in a space reserved for trucks, then slowly lowered himself down out of the cab and stretched. His stiff back cracked, reminding him longingly of the massage Rose had given him. He felt as if it had happened in another lifetime.

Maybe it had.

Stars still shone in the eastern sky, but a pale gray edge along the horizon announced the coming of day. Elko was barely two hours down the road. He groaned, rolling his shoulders and head to relax the tight muscles in his neck. Sleep. That's all he needed. Eight hours of uninterrupted, unworried sleep and he'd feel human again.

The door clicked on the passenger side. Ramsey walked around the front of the truck to help Rose. She still wore a guarded expression.

Ramsey regretted upsetting her. He really regretted the fact she knew he had a weapon. Hopefully, she didn't know where it was hidden.

After talking to Kat, he was definitely glad he'd brought the deadly thing along.

★ ★ ★

Rose grabbed her purse then climbed down out of the cab. She slung the strap over her shoulder and followed Ramsey across the broad expanse of parking lot. Another night on the road, another indistinguishable diner.

She couldn't help glancing from right to left, wondering who might lurk in the shadows. Ramsey'd thought she was asleep when the call came in. She'd distinctly heard him say Wendover would be a good place for the caller to 'catch up.'

He'd never have spoken so openly if he'd thought she was listening.

He'd called the person on the phone 'Kat.' The same woman he said he worked with, the one he'd been in contact with throughout the trip. So why would Handy Hannibal have been concerned about their whereabouts? Why hadn't Kat filled him in?

Did Ramsey and Kat even work for Hannibal Trucking? Was Handy's operation somehow involved in the hijackings?

And why were they talking about Yerington? There'd been at least one hijacking near there. Thieves, quite possibly the same ring that had been working the east coast, had recently stepped up their activity in the west, most noticeably in the desert area between Lovelock and Reno.

Ramsey'd mentioned the area's desolation. If he wasn't involved in the hijackings, why should he be so interested in an area totally off their route?

Following him into the diner, questioning his every move and reason, Rose still couldn't help but admire the way Ramsey commanded attention merely by his presence. Heads turned, both men's and women's. The faces of the men registered respect while the women openly ogled.

Rose shuddered. How could she feel so proud to be seen with Ramsey, to have people look at the two of them and assume they were a couple, and at the same time mistrust him?

Because I'm falling in love with a man who carries a gun, a man with secrets. A man brave enough to pull a stranger from a burning car, a man whose kisses turn my insides to jelly. A man hiding something.

Hiding something from me.

That's what hurt the most, Rose thought as she slid into the booth across from Ramsey. He'd asked for her trust then done everything in his power to destroy it.

He'd held her in his arms, said he cared about her, and she'd responded with honesty and passion.

She'd opened her heart and soul to Mike Ramsey.

His remained closed, locked behind a wall of dark secrets.

10

Elko, Nevada, Sunday evening

Rose scanned the crowded parking lot outside her motel room. Which one of the dozens of vehicles filling up the lot belonged to the elusive Kat? She tried to recall the cars she'd seen in Wendover, but none of these looked familiar. They'd made just a brief stop there, barely half an hour. Ramsey hadn't acted as if he expected someone.

He hadn't done anything at all suspicious, but Rose knew what she'd heard. Ramsey offering 'Kat' a chance to 'catch up.' Which meant the woman had obviously been following them all along.

But why? To arrange for a casual little hijacking . . . what else?

They'd arrived in Elko on schedule, found adjoining rooms and gone their separate ways. The walls were so thin, Rose had no doubt she'd have heard any phone calls or visitors Ramsey might have.

All she'd heard was a deep, repetitive rumble throughout the day, the sound of Ramsey snoring.

Sleep had eluded Rose. She'd washed her hair, brushed her hair, painted her fingernails, then her toenails. Anything to avoid crawling into that big empty bed, mere inches and a wall away from Ramsey.

She'd popped up to peek out the window whenever a car pulled into the lot, even though she had no idea who to look for. Finally, she gave up on sleep altogether, took a quick shower and called her aunt.

Rosa wasn't home.

Rose left a quick message on the answering machine. A knock sounded just as she hung up the phone.

'Ready?' Ramsey asked, when she unlocked the door.

He looked exhausted. Dark smudges shadowed his eyes and for the first time all week he hadn't bothered to shave. She wanted to touch his beard-roughened cheek and assure him everything was all right, the journey practically over.

Unfortunately, she couldn't do that. Everything wasn't all right. There were too many unanswered questions and over four hundred miles to travel tonight.

'I've got a full thermos of coffee and a couple of sandwiches already in the truck,' Ramsey said, stepping into the room.

'That'll be fine.' Rose slung her purse over

her shoulder, grabbed her sports bag, then shut the door behind her. She followed Ramsey out to the truck. They crossed the parking lot in silence.

Heavy clouds obscured the western sky, hiding the sunset and muting the rugged horizon as the big diesel rolled westward. The night grew darker, the tension inside the cab thicker with each mile traveled.

After a brief stop in Winnemucca, the highway curved south toward Lovelock. Rose stretched her arms and groaned as she arched her back.

'Do you want me to pull over so you can get out and stretch a bit?'

Ramsey's quiet offer startled Rose. He'd hardly spoken for the past hour. 'Yes, please,' she said, noticing once again how tired he looked. This week had been difficult for both of them, the past twenty-four hours especially hard.

The big rig shuddered to a noisy stop on a wide stretch of packed dirt, next to a pile of boulders well away from the highway. Ramsey climbed slowly out of the cab. 'I'm going to check the load,' he said. 'I want to make certain everything's secure before we head over the Sierras.'

Rose watched him disappear into the darkness, then climbed out of the cab.

Ramsey flipped open the cell phone and punched in Kat's number. One more thing to worry about. He hadn't been all that concerned when she didn't arrive in Wendover. It had been a quick stop, not much time for her to catch up. She should have contacted him in Elko, though, or at least called.

Her terse, 'Malone here,' calmed his fears. 'Where the hell are you?' he hissed. Her deep chuckle told him she saw right through his gruff question.

A few minutes later, Ramsey slipped the phone back into his pocket. *Car trouble.* He sighed and rubbed the tight muscles at the back of his neck. At least she'd found a rental and was doing her best to catch up.

He made a quick check of the load, then worked his way around to Rose's side of the truck. She stood outside, her arms reaching skyward. Ramsey stared as she arched her back and stretched, then leaned over and touched her toes before straightening up again to repeat the process.

The sight of her, clad in dark jeans and sweatshirt, her breasts swinging free beneath the heavy cotton as she gracefully swayed through her exercises, left a cold, hollow feeling in Ramsey's gut.

There was no use denying it any longer.

He'd gone and fallen in love.

He cleared his throat, not wanting to startle her, then stepped up behind Rose and softly kneaded the tight muscles at the base of her neck. Groaning, she leaned back into his touch and for a moment the tension of the past hours disappeared.

'How ya doin'?' he asked, working his thumbs along the planes of Rose's back.

'Mmmm, that feels wonderful. Oh, don't stop.'

'I don't want to stop.' Ramsey whispered against her ear, then trailed his lips along the line of her jaw until he tasted the sweet flesh at the base of her throat.

Rose turned slowly in his embrace and looped both arms over his shoulders. She rested her head against his chest. Her hair tickled his chin. 'I don't want you to stop either. But this isn't going to work, not this way.'

'We can make it work.' He cupped her face in his hands, searching her eyes for answers. Instead he saw only desperation and doubt.

And need. A need every bit as powerful as his own. Groaning, Ramsey captured Rose's mouth in his, tasting the fullness of her lips, nipping at the tender flesh inside, rejoicing in her passionate response.

She didn't want this, not with so many

questions unanswered between them, but there was no fighting the powerful surge of desire when Ramsey's lips touched hers, no way to control her almost manic craving for more.

His hands stroked her sides, then slipped inside her sweatshirt to caress her breasts. Her nipples hardened almost painfully, responding to the rough pads of his fingers as he rolled the tight little buds into points of pure sensation. He cupped her bottom and drew her up against his thighs. She felt the solid length and heat of his arousal, sensed the tightly leashed power. She strained against him, even as a small part of her mind acknowledged they had to stop, had to draw this wonderful torture to a close before they dropped right here in the sand and took each other by the side of the highway.

As Ramsey had said once before, this was neither the time nor the place. Sighing, Rose pulled away from his devastating kiss and rested her forehead against the solid wall of his chest. She sucked deep gulps of air into her lungs.

She heard the thunderous pounding in Ramsey's chest, felt the muscles expand like a deep bellows with each rush of air, as if he'd run a long, hard race. His chin rested gently on top of her bowed head, his hands gently stroked her sides.

A soft thunk startled her. Ramsey stiffened in her arms, then slid bonelessly along her body to the ground. Rose stared in mute horror as he rolled away, illuminated in the brilliant beam of a high-powered lantern, rolled away from her and onto his side, unconscious at her feet.

'Well, what have we here?' a familiar voice asked, invisible behind the blinding glare of the lamp. 'At least now I know why you gave my ring back.'

'James! What have you done? What are you doing here? My God, Ramsey.' Rose dropped to her knees and pressed her ear to Ramsey's chest, relieved to hear the steady beat of his heart.

'I might ask you the same thing, sweetheart,' James answered, sarcasm dripping from every word. 'Except I know exactly what you're doing here. Making love with a truck driver on the side of the road. You hardly know the man, Rose. He's definitely not your type. I find the whole affair disgusting.'

'How can you say that? Besides, what business is it of yours? Our engagement ended long before I gave your ring back. You have no right to come after me like some macho jerk. What if you'd killed him?' She turned her attention back to Ramsey, softly brushing the long dark hair back from his forehead. 'Ramsey? Please . . . wake up,' she pleaded.

'You think I'm out here because of him? Rose, don't be a fool. If you want to let some stranger fondle your breasts alongside a busy highway, that's your problem. I must admit, though, I'm surprised at how much you appear to enjoy it. You certainly never encouraged my attentions.' James reached for her.

Rose jerked away from him. 'You watched us? That's sick.' She pressed her hand to her stomach, fighting the sudden wave of nausea.

'We both did.' Tim Anderson stepped out of the shadows. 'You two put on quite a show.'

'Tim?' Rose looked from one familiar face to the other, her mind swirling with questions.

Suddenly, horribly, it all fell into place. Nausea gave way to white-hot anger. Tim and James, friends for years through thick and thin. James sticking up for Tim after his truck was hijacked, telling the head of Acme Insurance, Frank Bonner, that his old frat brother couldn't possibly be involved.

James, fascinated by her computer terminal, anxious to learn how to use *one of those things*, spending his time after hours while she worked, *playing* with her computer. Probably reading her files and recording the value and destination of every load insured through Rose's office.

Picking and choosing from his own supermarket of valuable commodities while she proudly stood by, offering her own head up on a platter. Enraged and humiliated, Rose sat back on her heels, gasping spasmodically for air.

'Figured it out, haven't you, Rose? I always thought you were a pretty smart girl.' Tim laughed as Rose struggled for control. 'In fact,' he added, 'it surprised me how easily James reeled you in. He's not known for his finesse with the women.'

'It's all connected, isn't it?' Rose asked, needing confirmation. 'The engagement, the wedding plans, all to keep me off balance. I can't believe I fell for it. You disgust me, both of you.' But not nearly as much as she disgusted herself. How could she have been so stupid?

'Rose, I . . . ' The subtle regret in James's voice surprised her.

'Why, James? It can't be the money. You have more than enough money, you have social standing, your family is highly respected in the community.' She suddenly thought of Alicia Dearborn and her many charities and social causes and almost felt sorry for the woman. 'Your mother will be . . . '

James blanched. Suddenly Rose understood.

'Your mother.' Rose shook her head in disgust. 'Oh, James,' she said, not trying to disguise her contempt. 'It all makes sense, in a sick sort of way. You finally managed to do something without Mother's permission!'

James turned aside, his action confirming Rose's accusation.

'Enough.' Tim reached down and hauled Rose to her feet, jerking her arm and bruising the tender flesh above her elbow. 'Time for true confessions later. Right now, we've got work to do.' Tim nudged Ramsey's body with the toe of his snakeskin boot. 'He's not going to stay out forever, no matter how appealing the concept might be.'

'You're right.' James bowed his head and turned away, then jogged into the darkness. He returned moments later with a length of nylon rope and proceeded to hog-tie Ramsey, hands behind his back, feet pulled tight and tied to the ropes at his wrists. Then he and Tim dragged Ramsey's inert body over against the boulders and left him there, face down in the dirt, out of sight of the highway.

Tim checked the knots and nodded his approval, then turned to Rose. 'Time to make a deal. His life for your cooperation.' He grinned at her. 'I'm not above inflicting a little pain on your truck driving paramour to help you make up your mind.'

Cooperate with thieves? Rose shuddered and wrapped her arms around herself in a protective gesture. This was all her fault. To think she'd actually suspected Ramsey. Why hadn't she listened to him? Why hadn't she been able to trust him?

'What do you want me to do?' Rose rubbed the sore flesh on her arm, painfully aware of how much Tim could hurt Ramsey while he lay there, helpless and unable to defend himself.

Tim stepped in front of Rose and set his flashlight on the gas tank at the side of the cab. The brilliant beam illuminated a swath of night before fading into nothingness. Rose stared along the course of the light, fighting the urge to back away from Tim. She knew instinctively the moment she showed him any weakness, she was lost.

He reached out and caressed her cheek with the backs of his fingers. The cold, dry touch of his knuckles against her flesh made her shiver. 'You're going to convince your truck driver that you are our leader. It shouldn't be too difficult for a smart girl like you.' He grinned, his teeth perfect and white.

She wanted to spit in his face. 'I don't think I'm interested.'

'You don't have any choice, remember? Unless you don't care what happens to him.' He nodded his head in Ramsey's direction. 'Besides, Rose, on paper you're already the boss. You have been, all along. When the walls come tumbling down, which they eventually always do, you're the one they're going to fall on. We just never expected you to step into position quite so nicely. That's been the hard part, you see, trying to figure out how we were going to turn the operation over to you in time for the rest of us to leave the country.

'Of course, the key is convincing Ramsey you're the chief thief, so to speak. When he's rescued, he'll be more than willing to point the finger at you. We figure that'll keep the Feds tied up long enough for the rest of us to take advantage of some very well planned vacations.'

'I haven't done anything,' Rose said, her voice laced with all the contempt she could muster. 'Even if Ramsey thinks I'm guilty, there's no real proof.'

'You can plead your innocence as loud and long as you like, but it won't help. You've heard the term 'paper trail,' haven't you? Well, we've laid one that leads right to your doorstep. It'll make things more pleasant for all of us if you cooperate.'

'Why should I?' Rose glanced in Ramsey's direction, seeing nothing more than a still, dark mound against the boulders.

Tim pinched her chin painfully between his thumb and forefinger, turning her face back to his, forcing her to look directly into his eyes. Feral eyes, she suddenly realized. The eyes of a killer. 'Don't make me repeat myself. I told you. I will hurt him. Badly. Maybe I won't kill him. He might prefer it, though. No matter. When I'm done he's going to blame you, so you might as well go along.'

His fingers tightened against her flesh and Rose barely suppressed a moan of pain. Suddenly James's voice spilled out of the darkness. Rose hadn't been aware of him standing quietly in the shadows while Tim voiced his ugly threats. 'Why don't you take it easy on her,' James asked in a reasonable tone of voice. 'If you hurt her, she can't cooperate.'

Tim wavered a moment, as if loath to allow James the chance to make a decision, then finally loosened his grip and nodded his head in agreement. Rose let out the breath she hadn't realized she'd been holding and waited to see what would come next.

'Get in the truck, Rose.'

She didn't question James's quiet command.

Once inside, Rose breathed a sigh of relief and slumped against the leather seat. How could this have happened? She felt numb, her mind incapable of functioning beyond her immediate fears. And to think she'd suspected Ramsey!

She couldn't, wouldn't think about him lying out there, unconscious. She'd heard his heart beat, felt his chest rise and fall, but what if he was badly injured? She hadn't seen any blood, but James and Tim hadn't given her a chance to examine him carefully, either. Ramsey was going to be okay. She wouldn't allow herself to consider the alternative.

Tim frightened her. When he talked about hurting Ramsey his eyes glowed in feverish delight. James, at least, had appeared to hang back while Tim made his threats. Probably trying to figure out how he was going to explain all this to his therapist.

Or his mother.

Rose hadn't noticed a cruel streak in James. She hadn't seen it before in Tim, either, but she hadn't known him as well as she'd known James.

Or thought she'd known James. Lord, she'd been engaged to one of the hijackers all along! Ramsey would never forgive her. Well, she'd have plenty of time to think about how stupid and gullible she'd been, because she'd probably spend the rest of her life in prison.

'Had time to consider our offer?' Tim must have jumped up on the step, because he was suddenly only inches away, staring at Rose through the partially opened window. She noticed tiny specks of saliva at the corners of his lips and shuddered. He made her think of a rabid weasel.

'Yes.'

'Then get out here. I think your boyfriend's coming to. I don't want him to have any doubts about your part, or the deal's off.'

'He won't.' Rose choked back the tears that suddenly filled her throat and threatened to spill from her eyes. Ramsey was an innocent victim in this mess, a truck driver just trying to do his job. She'd do anything necessary to protect him, then worry about herself later.

For one brief moment, Rose thought of the tender, passionate embrace she and Ramsey had shared. Under the watchful eyes of Tim Anderson and James Dearborn.

A white-hot rush of frustration and anger filled her. She had one option, and only one. Play her role to the hilt, take whatever humiliation was heaped upon her, and convince Ramsey she led this gang of thieves.

That should save him.

Of course, it would also make him hate her.

★ ★ ★

Ramsey knew he'd heard a man's angry voice, but how could that be? He'd been making love to Rose, the two of them stretched out on a sandy beach, all alone with only the seabirds to keep them company. If only his head didn't hurt so damned much! He tried to roll over, then tried again as consciousness seeped slowly into the pounding space behind his eyes.

When he tried to straighten his legs and couldn't, reality slammed him right in the chest. His hands were tied, expertly by the feel of the tight knots, his feet drawn up against the backs of his thighs. A cramp threatened one leg.

Rose! Where was she? He remembered kissing her, reveling in the feel of loving her, then suddenly, nothing. He tried to raise his head and managed a very slight shift in his position.

It was more than enough.

What he saw made him wish that whatever blow had knocked him out had killed him instead.

Illuminated by the powerful beam of a

199

large lantern, Rose leaned against the truck, conversing with someone who could only be James Dearborn. Next to them stood the man from the diner. Ramsey recognized Tim Anderson immediately. Obviously he hadn't checked into that hotel in Bermuda after all.

It had been there all along, in the DOT reports Ramsey had studied. The first hijacking, a load of goods hauled by Tim Anderson. Dearborn had helped get him off the hook. Rose was the link at Acme. Why hadn't he made the connection?

Ramsey groaned and lowered his face back down onto the hard packed dirt. He'd been right to suspect Rose. She was involved all right, all the way up to her pretty neck. From the way the two men appeared to defer to her, she must be in charge of the whole damned ring. Just as he'd suspected in the very beginning. Why hadn't he trusted his instincts in the first place?

Because he'd fallen in love with a thief. He'd let his damned gonads do his thinking for him, had pushed every logical conclusion and obvious clue out the window. To top it off, he'd listened to Kathleen. As if she was some great expert on love. *Ha!* The woman hadn't had a date in three years.

But he'd believed in Rose. He'd believed in her goodness, he'd even begun to trust her.

He'd told her he cared for her, something he'd never told another woman. Thank goodness he hadn't said he loved her.

Ramsey didn't know whether he wanted to cry or just kill her. Where the hell was Kathleen? He'd kill his partner while he was at it. If he ever got the stupid ropes untied.

'You awake, Ramsey?' Anderson hunkered down next to him. 'We just wanted to let you know we'll be relieving you of your trailer and that lovely scraper you've hauled all the way out here for us. Rose said to let you keep the truck. It's an old model, not worth much. I considered taking it, but you know Rose. Whatever the boss wants, she gets.' The flashlight beam blinded Ramsey, the pain in the back of his head made him feel as if his skull was about to explode.

It wasn't nearly as bad as the pain in his heart.

'I want to talk to Rose.'

'It's up to her.' Tim stood up and gestured toward Rose. 'Hey Rose, honey. Your truck driver wants a word with you.'

He couldn't see her as she came up behind him, but Ramsey was aware of Rose's presence with every fiber of his being.

'You wanted to talk to me?' Her voice sounded cold and stiff. Nothing like his sweet Rose. Nothing at all.

'You mean you don't have anything to say?' Ramsey laughed, a harsh sound as he saw himself as she must see him, hog-tied, face down in the dirt. Humiliated and beaten. What a fool he'd been. A damned, lovesick fool.

'No, I guess I don't,' Rose said quietly. He heard the crunch of gravel beneath her boots as she turned and walked away.

'You're just going to leave me here?'

'Yeah, Ramsey, I am. Maybe that woman you keep talking to on the phone will come to your rescue. I doubt you'll be out here all that long.'

Woman? She must mean Kat. He tried to think of what Rose might have overheard. Had he gotten sloppy and tipped her off?

'C'mon. That's enough.' Anderson leaned over and patted Ramsey on the shoulder as he left. 'I really feel terrible about this, you know,' he whispered in a conspiratorial tone. 'We should have waited a few more minutes, given you the time to get a little, if you know what I mean. She's a hot little number. Poor James, though. He was getting anxious. It wouldn't have been fair.' He straightened up, moving out of Ramsey's field of vision. 'Bye now, Mr. Ramsey. Enjoy your evening.'

Ramsey sagged against his bonds, beyond anger, beyond pain. He couldn't possibly feel heartache over her lies. There was no heart left in him. That place in his chest that had responded to every word Rose said, every touch, every glance, that place was gone, ripped clean away.

He really was gonna kill Kathleen. She'd encouraged him, told him Rose was good and kind and worth loving. He'd fallen in love with a crook, a two-timing crook if her proximity to her so-called ex-fiancé meant anything.

Where the hell was Kathleen, anyway? She'd had plenty of time to catch up. In fact, if she'd been where she was supposed to be, she would have caught him with his hand on Rose's breast. He clenched his jaw in renewed anger. How could he have been so stupid?

The rumble of a big diesel engine shattered the night. Steel rasped against steel as someone unhitched the trailer and dropped the bar. A few minutes later, a different truck rolled into view.

Transferring the trailer from one rig to another took a surprisingly short time, proof to Ramsey the hijackers had done this often. He tried to count how many men were involved, but his eyes kept straying to Rose. She stood just within Ramsey's line of sight, cool, aloof, gorgeous as ever.

He struggled against the bonds, twisting his hands in a futile effort to reach the knots with his fingers. By the time the tractor-trailer rolled out onto the road, his wrists were slippery with blood.

A sedan pulled up next to him, the engine idled quietly. Ramsey tried to raise his head to see if Rose was in the car, but all he saw was the bottom half of Dearborn's face as he leaned out the open window. 'What do you want now, Dearborn?' The foul taste of bile rose in his throat. He'd never felt the desire to kill before now. It wasn't a pleasant sensation.

'I am sorry to leave you like this,' Dearborn said, 'but there are things happening here that are out of my control. I have Rose, and I'll keep her safe. Things are not always what they seem, Ramsey.'

'I could care less what happens to Rose DeAngelo,' Ramsey spat. 'But I will find you, Dearborn. I will find you and you will regret you ever knew me. Do you understand, Dearborn?'

There was no answer. Ramsey didn't expect one. What he got was a face full of gravel when the car sped away.

He tugged futilely at the ropes, ignoring the pain. Where the hell was Kathleen? She'd been in Winnemucca when he'd called, barely a half hour from here. He'd been tied up a damn sight longer than thirty minutes.

A sudden cramp ripped through the big muscle in his upper thigh. Ramsey gasped with pain, straining rigidly against the ropes that bound him. The muscle contracted tighter. In frustration and anger, he called out for his partner.

But the name he screamed was *Rose*.

★ ★ ★

Rose refused to look at James and she knew if Ramsey slipped into her thoughts she would die. Instead, she stared blankly out the side window as the Mercedes sped across the desert.

'I'm sorry I got you into this, Rose.'

'What?' She spun around in her seat, stunned by James's quiet apology. 'It's a little late for that, don't you think?'

'I never meant it to go this far, to involve you like this.'

'Why, James?' Finally, she let her anger surface. 'The thefts are bad enough. You used me, set me up. But why a marriage proposal? Did you need to humiliate me even more?'

'Bonner ordered it. I had no choice but to do as he said.'

'Bonner? Frank Bonner, the company president?'

205

'One and the same.' James glanced in her direction, his face empty of expression. There was nothing there for her to read, no sign of his thoughts. Why tell her all this? Did he intend to kill her, after all?

'Remember the first theft? Bonner had every right to be suspicious. Tim hijacked his own shipment. I was in on it. He had financial trouble, gambling debts mostly. I'd been loaning him money, pulling it out of one of Mother's accounts. When he couldn't pay it back I panicked. She'd threatened to disinherit me once before. I knew if Mother found out I'd been stealing from her, well . . . it seemed like a good idea at the time.'

Rose didn't comment, afraid once she did, he'd stop talking.

James drove carefully, both hands gripping the wheel. She'd always thought his hands were beautiful, the hands of an artist, almost feminine. Small, perfectly formed, the nails neatly manicured. She concentrated on his hands. It was easier than looking at his face.

'We thought we were so smart.' He cleared his throat, then continued. 'Tim set everything up, even hit himself over the head because I couldn't do it.' James laughed then, a harsh, humorless sound. 'Did such a good job, he's still got the scar. Serves him right. Thank goodness he'd already taught me how to drive a truck. I had to get the rig off the highway while he lay there unconscious. I hid it in an abandoned barn that belonged to the parents of a frat brother. He helped us fence the stuff later. If I'd only known then . . . '

He didn't say anything for awhile. Rose waited, finally giving in to impatience. 'Where does Mr. Bonner come into this?'

'Bonner? He figured out we'd done it. Didn't take him long. Tim got a little greedy and the goods started turning up on the black market too soon after the theft. Bonner was watching for the stuff.'

'So why didn't he turn you in?'

'Hijacking's more profitable, and black-mail's extremely effective when properly applied.'

'He's blackmailing you? You and Tim both?'

'No, just me. Tim loves what he's doing. He thinks Frank Bonner is wonderful, paying him to steal and beat up on people. Tim's in his element. I never realized before how cruel he is. That's why I've got you with me, Rose. I don't like the way he watches you. He makes me nervous.'

She struggled to control the shudder that zipped across her shoulders. Tim made her a lot more than nervous. He scared her to death. 'Why should you care, James? What's it matter to you?' She didn't try to disguise her bitterness.

'Whether you believe it or not, it does matter and I do care. It's my fault you're involved in the first place.' The silence stretched on into the darkness, disturbed only by the steady hum of the powerful motor. James's voice was barely above a whisper when he spoke again. 'Remember how we met?'

'Of course.' How could she forget? A couple of toughs had hassled her one morning before work. One of the handsomest men she'd ever seen had rushed to her aid. She remembered feeling as if she'd been rescued by a blond James Bond.

'Tim paid those two guys to give you a bad time, then to back off when I showed up. It worked. You agreed to go out with me.'

Horrified, Rose listened in silence as James spelled out how easily she had been duped. What a fool she'd been.

'It was a simple plan. I date the insurance adjuster for a couple of weeks before the robbery. Then we'd have a sympathetic person at the agency in case there were any problems. It was all Tim's idea, to date you, then break up with you once the claim was settled. I certainly didn't intend to make truck hijackings a career. Mother would never approve.'

You're kidding, right? she wanted to shout. *Mother would never approve? How truly sad for you, James.*

'Bonner had other ideas. After he got involved and informed us we were now business partners, he ordered me to get closer to you. You had the information and you were the perfect scapegoat. I didn't have a choice in the matter. Besides, being engaged to you kept Mother off my back. Until she wanted to start planning the wedding. That made me nervous. I was actually relieved when you gave the ring back, especially with her there as a witness. Now she feels sorry for me.'

'Gee, that positively makes my day,' Rose said, shocked she almost saw the humor in James's situation. 'You certainly do a lot for my ego.'

'I am sorry, Rose.' He glanced in her direction, remorse written in the set of his jaw and the pain in his eyes. 'I grew to care for you a great deal, but all the time I was courting you, I was using you. I'll always regret we didn't meet under better circumstances.'

'I think it's a little late for regrets, don't you? Unless you intend to help me get out of this.' A pale glimmer of hope raised her spirits.

'I've thought about it, believe me. The

problem is, the Feds'll still think you're guilty. Bonner's good at what he does, shuffling paper in creative ways. He's set it up so that it all points to you.'

'If you give yourself up and explain everything, they'll believe you.'

'Think about it, Rose. If I do that, I'll go to prison. With my looks, do you honestly think I'd survive?'

He turned back to her, a combination of fear and distaste marring his patrician features. No, Rose had to admit, James Dearborn would have a very rough time of it in prison.

That didn't mean she wouldn't do her best to send him there.

11

It was almost three o'clock Monday morning by the time James pulled the big Mercedes up to a nondescript warehouse near an abandoned copper mine somewhere between Fallon and Yerington. Road-weary to the point of numbness, Rose watched him punch a series of buttons on the dash. A large door silently opened, then closed just as smoothly behind them as the Mercedes slipped quietly through the entrance.

Rose tried to remember the sequence of numbers he'd used, but the memory fled in the blinding flash of brilliant overhead lights. She blinked a couple of times before she was able to focus on the cavernous interior of the building. Huge crates and boxes filled one end. Half a dozen men in matching blue coveralls operated forklifts and cranes, loading material into a massive camouflage-painted Chinook helicopter.

'I don't believe this,' Rose muttered. Who would have ever thought something like this . . .

'Quiet.' James glanced briefly in her direction, the tension in him obvious in the tight clenching of his jaw, the slight tremor in his hands.

Rose looked away, overwhelmed by the scope of activity surrounding them.

James parked the car next to a couple of nondescript sedans. Rose immediately spotted the scraper Ramsey had been hauling. The enormous earth moving monster sat partially stripped, already in the process of dismantling by another group of identically clad workers. 'So this is how you move the equipment,' Rose said. Suddenly it all made sense. 'You break everything down so it can't be identified, then move it out of the country. That's what's been so frustrating, not knowing what happened to all the stolen trucks and equipment, not being able to figure out where it was all going.'

'Quit talking,' James ordered. 'The less they think you actually know . . . ' He let the sentence dangle.

Rose shut her mouth. But her eyes stayed open . . . wide.

Other partially disassembled pieces of machinery lined another wall. She counted a total of at least two dozen workers, including the ones crawling about the metal hulks with welding torches and monkey wrenches in a scene reminiscent of an old James Bond thriller.

She watched in stunned silence, vaguely aware of hysterical laughter lurking somewhere close to the surface. *They expect the Feds to believe I'm running this? Me?* This operation appeared larger, more organized and expansive than the capabilities of some Third World countries!

'In your dreams,' she muttered, unfastening the seat belt and climbing stiffly out of the car.

'What did you say?' James got out, shut his door and stretched.

'Nothing James. You wouldn't understand.' She'd worked so damned hard for her promotion to division manager, done everything she was asked, all honest and above-board to keep her little part of the company intact and running smoothly. How ironic to think she'd probably end up in prison, convicted of masterminding an illegal operation so complex she couldn't begin to understand it.

'Hey Dearborn, we've got a big problem.' Suddenly Tim stepped out of the shadows and grabbed James's arm. Obviously the move was meant to startle. James merely looked Tim up and down with a supercilious sneer and backed away.

His attitude didn't seem to faze Tim. Rose had the feeling the two men had played their little power games for years. She wondered if they were really friends at all. As if reading her mind, Tim leered over his shoulder at Rose. His gaze swept her from head to toe, and back again. She shivered uncontrollably at the salacious expression on his face.

'What now, Tim?' James stepped in front of Rose, blocking Tim's view. The sympathetic gesture offered Rose a thread of hope. Somehow she had to convince James to help her escape. She had to get back to Ramsey, make certain he was all right.

'Our friend Ramsey's no truck driver. Bonner found out he's a DOT investigator working on — ya want the drum roll? This case.'

Rose sagged against the Mercedes as both James and Tim turned to glare at her. Ramsey, an investigator with the Department of Transportation? Had everything he'd said to her, done with her, been a lie? She held her hand across her middle, afraid she might be sick.

'I'd guess from the look on your face you didn't know,' James said. Before Rose could answer, Tim interrupted.

'That's not what Bonner thinks. He says she's in on the investigation. The scraper was a setup. They changed the assigned route without telling anyone but you, Dearborn. As

I recall, the lady here slipped that bit of useful information your way.' He sneered at Rose. 'Which pretty much narrows down the list of suspects.'

'Is that true, Rose?' James's classic features twisted in an ugly scowl. 'Did you set us up?'

'No. I didn't know anything, believe me.' Why couldn't the ground just open up and swallow her? 'I thought he was a truck driver, just an ordinary truck driver. For awhile, I actually suspected him . . . I thought he . . . I had no idea . . . ' Ramsey didn't tell anyone about the route change? Only Rose? And Rose told James. Was she the one Ramsey was after? Good God, no wonder he'd accepted her guilt so easily! *Take a number, fellas*, she wanted to shout. *Ramsey set me up, too.*

'Right,' Tim snarled. 'Like I really believe you're not involved. Bonner thinks he's so smart. It's almost funny to think you've been a step ahead of him all along.' He laughed, an ugly sound without humor. 'It should be interesting to see what he does next. I mean, I know what I'd do, but Frank hates to get his hands dirty. C'mon, let's go.'

She had to stay calm. If only her hands would stop trembling! Somehow, she had to help Ramsey.

Even though he'd lied. The laughter, the loving, the kisses that curled her toes, all lies.

She'd been scammed every bit as successfully as the hijackers.

Her anger grew as she followed Tim and James up a flight of stairs. James had lied, Ramsey had lied, even her boss had been lying to her! By the time she reached Frank Bonner's office it was all she could do to control her rage. *Men!* She glared at the backs of the two ahead of her.

Bonner, visible behind the glassed wall of his office, held the phone to his ear with one hand and pounded on the desk with the other. His face contorted in anger and Rose had a strange sense of dèja vú. He'd been arguing with someone over the phone last Monday, in an office similar to this the day she'd walked out.

One week ago.

Only this time, he looked up and saw her. Without another word, he slammed the phone back in its cradle and threw open the door.

'What the hell did you bring the bitch here for?' he demanded. Even Tim backed away. 'You idiots! What were you thinking?'

James pulled Rose to one side, putting himself between her and Frank. Once again, she had the sense he was protecting her, although his action had been so subtle no one else appeared to notice the shift in their positions.

'You told us to tie up the truck driver, steal the rig, and make it look like she was the mastermind. That's what we did,' James said. 'Ramsey's convinced she's in charge of the whole operation. We couldn't very well tie her up too, not if she's supposed to be our boss.'

'You could have gotten rid of her once you were out of his sight. I can't believe this little fool actually thought she could put one over on me. Me!' He slammed his fist against the desk and spun away from Rose. 'What a mess you idiots are making of this. Luckily one of the men spotted Ramsey's partner in Winnemucca, or you and your little fraternity brother here would be in handcuffs by now. I can't believe how incompetent you are.'

Kat. The woman who'd called, the one Ramsey said he worked with. She must be the partner Frank meant. 'What did you do to her,' Rose asked, remembering the warmth in the woman's voice. The life. 'Did you . . . '

'Unfortunately I don't know,' Bonner said, taking a deep breath and rubbing the back of his neck. 'Hal said he thunked her on the head and she dropped like a rock. He left her locked in the trunk of her car in the parking lot, but the bitch might still be alive. This is all coming down too fast,' he muttered, addressing Tim. 'We need to get the goods loaded and out of here by dawn. What you can't get in the chopper, take out on flatbeds and head south. I'm putting you in charge and I don't want any more screw-ups.'

He turned away from Tim, effectively dismissing him. 'You,' he said to Rose, 'present a bigger problem.' He glared at James. 'The fact she's in on this with Ramsey ruins everything. This makes the evidence I've spent the better part of two years planting completely worthless!'

'She says she didn't know Ramsey was with the DOT.'

'Shut up, Dearborn. This is your fault. I've got too much invested in this operation to let her ruin it. Lock her in the staff room. I'll have one of the crew take care of her after we're out of here. Now get out.' He turned away, mumbling as he reached for the phone.

Rose thought she heard him say something about taking care of 'that blasted investigator,' too. *Ramsey!*

She bowed her head and briefly shut her eyes. No matter what he believed of her, she couldn't bear the thought of harm coming to him. She loved him. Somehow, some way, she had to save him.

It was up to her. She had to think of something, some way out of this, but her mind refused to function. *Too much, too fast.* James grabbed her by the upper arm and led her away. Frank spoke tersely into the phone as they left. Arranging their murders?

Blindly she followed James. Down the flight of stairs, across the huge warehouse, each step taking her closer to the single doorway on the far side of the building. James hadn't said a word, Rose couldn't. Her lips were frozen, her feet moved automatically.

Suddenly James jerked Rose's arm, pulling her behind one of the large stacks of crates. She stumbled, fell against him, almost cried out. 'What are you doing?' she hissed, grabbing his arm for support.

'I am not a killer.' James looked away from Rose. 'I may be a thief and a coward, but I am not a killer. Rose, I didn't mean for this to happen, I had no idea it would come to this . . .'

'Then help me,' Rose begged. 'Help me get out of here.'

'I can't, Rose. God, I don't know what to do.' He turned to face her then, wild-eyed and frantic.

'Listen,' Rose said, trying to keep her hopes in check and the desperation out of her voice. If she could only convince him . . . 'You're all gonna get caught. You're not going to get away with this, not with Ramsey on to you. Let me go, then call the police. Turn Frank and Tim in to the authorities and give yourself up. You know the Feds'll need a witness. You can strike a deal, James. I know you can. You'll probably end up spending a couple of months in one of those ritzy Federal prisons. They're just country clubs in disguise. You won't do hard time, not when the authorities learn Frank was blackmailing you.'

She could barely contain herself when James turned to her with a glimmer of hope on his face.

'Do you think so?' He grabbed Rose by the shoulders, forced her to look directly into his pale blue eyes. She held his gaze and prayed for inspiration.

'Rose, I never meant to hurt you. You don't deserve any of this . . . but I am so afraid.' He released her shoulders and raised his hands as if in supplication. 'I don't know what to do, Rose. I've never seen Bonner this angry.' His whisper exploded into a hoarse shout. 'What should I do?'

'Shhhh!' Rose pressed her fingers against James's lips. She stuck her head around the side of the crate. What if someone heard him? No one even glanced in their direction.

Rose slumped against the crate. What now?

Don't be a twit — take advantage of the situation.

Wasn't that what Aunt Rosa would say?

From experience, Rose knew she'd be a fool not to heed her aunt's advice.

She placed her free hand on James's arm and gave him a comforting squeeze. 'James, I've never seen Frank Bonner this upset, either. I think he's really lost it. You heard him, didn't you? He blames you. Knowing Frank, I can assure you, he won't forgive you when this all falls apart. He won't let you out of this alive. I've seen the man lose his temper before, and that was in a civilized setting where he had to behave. There's no one here to tell him how to act. He makes his own rules.'

James stared at her, a deep, penetrating gaze. Rose gave him a moment to consider what she'd said, then tightened her grip on his arm. 'You haven't got a thing to lose by helping me. If you lock me in that room, you might as well add murder to your list of charges. That is, if you live long enough to be charged with the murder of an unarmed woman.'

She watched his expression as the implications of what she'd said sunk in. After a moment that stretched into eternity, James sighed and shrugged. 'Okay, Rose. You've got all the answers,' he said. 'What do we do now?'

Good question. 'We leave.' She smiled at

him, projecting as much calm and confidence as she could muster under the circumstances. 'We're going to walk across the floor and get in the car. Everyone here's so busy, they won't pay any attention to us.'

'You can guarantee that, right?' The faintest glimmer of a grin tilted the corner of his lips, but did nothing to disguise the fear in his eyes.

'Of course.' She stuck her head around the side of the crate. If anything, activity in the warehouse had grown even more frenetic. 'It's now or never,' she whispered, tugging on James's sleeve. 'Let's go.'

'Your call.' He looped his arm around her waist and walked her casually across the broad expanse of open floor.

Anyone looking their way would see a couple strolling comfortably down the length of the warehouse. James's fingers trembled spasmodically against Rose's waist.

They reached the car and James guided Rose to the driver's side of the Mercedes, then opened the door. 'You drive,' he said, and handed her the keys. 'If I'm gonna do this, I'm gonna do it right. There's a pay phone just down the road. Drop me off there and I'll call the police.' He smiled softly at Rose, a sad, lost smile that made her heart break. 'If you hurry,' he said, 'you might be able to get to your truck driver in time.'

Rose slid behind the wheel and buckled her seat belt. James climbed into the seat next to her and she eased the big car up to the closed door. 'All right, James. Punch in the code.'

'I just did.'

'The door didn't open.'

'I'm aware of that. Let me try it again.' James frantically punched a series of numbers.

Nothing happened.

'C'mon, James.' Rose glanced in the rearview mirror. A sudden movement caught her eye. She adjusted the mirror for a clearer view across the warehouse.

Frank Bonner stood just outside his office talking to Tim and another man. The Mercedes sat in plain view of his position.

If he looked this way . . .

'Something's not right,' James muttered. 'I'll have to open it manually.'

'Don't let them see you,' Rose warned. 'They're up on the walkway.'

James quietly slipped out of the car.

'Please hurry,' Rose begged, unable to take her eyes off Frank and Tim. They seemed to be arguing, but at least they were totally involved in each other. Rose wondered if her pounding heart might not be loud enough to give them away.

'Let's go,' James ordered, appearing suddenly

beside her in the front seat. 'It won't stay open long.'

In fact, the big door had already begun its long slide back to the ground. Rose threw the Mercedes into gear, thankful for the noisy activity in the warehouse and the quiet engine as they barely cleared the bottom edge of the door and sped into the night.

She didn't turn on the headlights until they reached the main road, almost a quarter of a mile away. A road that would lead her to the highway and back to Ramsey. James pointed to a phone booth. Rose slammed on the brakes. The car skidded to a halt.

James started to open the door, then paused. 'Rose . . . ' He leaned over and kissed her, very gently, on the cheek. 'I am sorry, Rose. Will you ever be able to forgive me?'

'You call the police, like you promised,' she said, reaching out to touch his arm. 'Tell them what's going on, what Frank Bonner has done to you, to all of us. I'll forgive you and if you need me, I promise to be there for you. I'll testify how you helped me.'

'Thank you.' He slipped quickly out of the car. 'Now hurry.'

She watched as he stepped up to the phone booth, lifted the receiver off the hook and punched in a series of three numbers. He waved to her as she gunned the powerful engine and sped into the night.

★ ★ ★

The horizon was beginning to glow in the east, pale blue fading into navy by the time Ramsey felt the first strands of rope begin to separate.

He'd been rubbing the piece connecting his wrists to his ankles against the edge of one of those damned boulders all night long, but the rock kept crumbling beneath the stiff rope. Fresh and drying blood covered his hands and wrists. He hated to imagine the flies and other noxious things that might be drawn by the scent once the sun rose over the horizon.

Of course, he'd just be trading one set of critters for another. The ones that had crawled over and around him throughout the long dark hours would soon give up and go home, making way for the second shift.

Nothing had bitten him yet, but something with lots of legs was currently working its way across his throat, making it difficult to concentrate on the precise movements necessary to wear through his bonds. It wasn't easy, hog-tied with ankles and wrists pulled together behind him, to find one particular strand of rope and work it long enough and hard enough against a crumbly piece of sandstone until it frayed through. It took complete and total concentration.

Which, in a way, made Ramsey thankful for the bugs and the cramps in his legs and back and the searing pain where the ropes had torn through his flesh. He had to concentrate even harder to do the job.

That kept his mind off Rose.

He'd certainly learned an important lesson. Until now he hadn't known the first thing about hatred. At some point during the long, lonely hours he'd realized you had to have an emotional investment in a person before you could really and truly hate them.

All things considered, he decided he really and truly hated Rose DeAngelo.

Something stung him just beneath his jaw and Ramsey jerked, shouting an oath. Then he sighed and cursed again, this time with relief. He'd snapped the weakened rope. His hands were still tied together behind him, but for the first time in hours Ramsey could straighten his legs, even though his ankles also remained tightly bound.

He rolled over onto his back, his legs numb and burning at the same time from the sudden return of circulation. After a few moments he eased himself into a sitting position against the boulders, then scooted against the rock until he was on his feet, swaying slightly and panting with the effort.

Even with his hands and feet tied, Ramsey figured he could easily make the twenty or so yards to the truck. Once he got there it shouldn't take more than a few minutes rubbing against the sharp metal bumper to cut through the ropes binding his wrists.

He hopped, covering about ten inches, then swayed to keep balance. The sky grew lighter, making it easier to see the uneven spots on the ground that might trip him.

He hopped again, and then again, wobbling at each awkward landing. His throat itched where he'd been stung. He rubbed his neck against his shoulder, missed the itch completely, swayed, cursed, overbalanced, then did a perfect face plant into the dust.

Groaning, Ramsey considered sliding along the ground on his belly, but he figured he'd probably die of old age before he got to the truck. Finally, he rolled over and sat up so he could scoot across the uneven surface on his rear end.

He was halfway to the rig, pulling himself along with his heels, pushing with his butt and the tips of his fingers when Kathleen pulled in. Her car skidded to a halt, throwing sand and rock in all directions.

'Where the hell have you been?' he bellowed, masking his relief. He must look like a damned fool, scooting across the ground on his butt. He sure as hell wasn't going to let her write up this report.

Kathleen crawled unsteadily out of the car, took a long look at Ramsey and doubled over in hysterics.

'What the hell's so damned funny?' he asked. 'Get your sweet fanny over here and untie me. Now!'

'Have a little sympathy, old man.' She wiped her eyes and pushed the long fall of blond hair back from her face. Even in the pale light of dawn, Ramsey could see the bloody contusion that covered half of her forehead and blackened her right eye.

'Lord, Kat, what . . . ?

'I had a really bad night, Ramsey, okay?' She groaned when she leaned over to grab the knife out of her boot. 'But it looks like I fared better than you. Where's your woman?'

'Not one word about that lying bitch,' he snarled, then leaned over so Kathleen could cut the ropes binding his hands. The sharp blade slipped through the strands as if they were butter. Kathleen flipped the weapon around and handed it to Ramsey so he could free his own legs. She plopped down in the sand next to him and leaned against his shoulder.

'She's in on it, eh?' Kathleen turned to look at Ramsey through the matted blood in her hair.

'In on it? Hell, she's in charge. I feel like a complete idiot, the way that woman played me. Which reminds me, what happened to you?'

'I stopped in Winnemucca for coffee and some yahoo caught me out in the parking lot. I don't know what he hit me with, but I woke up a few hours later in the trunk of my car with the mother of all headaches. It took me awhile to jimmy the latch on the trunk, then I had to hot-wire the car. The bug on the scraper indicates it's somewhere out near Yerington, but I had a hunch I'd find you with the truck.'

Kathleen took a deep breath and touched Ramsey's shoulder in a gesture of apology. 'Sorry I took so long to get here. I feel like this is all my fault. I told you to trust her. I can't believe how wrong I was.'

'Don't blame yourself. I'm the one who screwed up.' Ramsey handed Kathleen's knife back to her and crawled unsteadily to his feet. He held out a hand to help her up and the two of them wobbled over to the truck and sat on the running board.

'What now?' Kathleen asked.

'We get you to a hospital and get that head of yours checked.'

'I'm okay. You know how hard-headed I am.'

'I won't argue that, but I want a doctor to confirm your diagnosis.'

'What about you?' She reached over and lifted one of his hands. 'You're bleeding all over yourself.'

'First aid kit's in the cab,' Ramsey said. 'I'll get it and you can patch me up. I'd hate to mess up Handy's new leather upholstery.' He opened the door and climbed up on the step. The first aid kit was just inside the door, tucked away in a small compartment.

As he reached for it, a dark gray Mercedes pulled into the turnout on the opposite side of the truck from Ramsey and skidded to a halt.

Dearborn's car.

'Kat,' he hissed. 'Cover.'

He crawled across the seat and peered over the edge of the open passenger window. The morning sun reflected off the tinted windows on the Mercedes. Ramsey had no idea how many passengers the large vehicle held. He slid back across the seat and reached down beside the door to flip a second latch, one hidden beneath the first aid kit. Carefully Ramsey removed his revolver.

He slid back across the leather seat, ignoring the trail of blood staining Handy's newly recovered cushions. He glanced behind him in time to see Kathleen crawl up on the step and move around the back of the cab, out of sight of anyone in the Mercedes, but close enough to offer back-up. She carried a lethal looking 9mm automatic pistol in her right hand.

Ramsey wiped his bloody hands across his denim clad thighs to secure a cleaner grip, then quietly pulled the hammer back on the revolver. His hands were steady as he positioned himself out of sight in the cab, but with a clear view of the Mercedes.

He trained the gun on the driver's side door and waited for it to open.

★   ★   ★

Rose turned off the key in the ignition and grabbed the steering wheel with both hands, then rested her forehead across the top. She was too late. The plain gray sedan parked near the pile of boulders had to mean Frank's hired gun had beaten her to Ramsey.

But where was he? Where was his killer? Rose knew if she was smart she'd leave, leave now and get as far away from everything as she could. She'd have to change her name and start a new life, but she'd be alive.

But what kind of life would it be without Ramsey?

The silence was unnerving. She raised her head, looking once again in the direction of the strange sedan. It didn't look like a killer's car. In fact, it had a rental sticker on the bumper.

Could Ramsey's partner be alive? Had she reached him first? They could both be here, somewhere. Ramsey and Kat. Rose felt a sudden twist of jealousy when she thought of Ramsey's partner, a woman he worked with. A woman he trusted. Would he ever trust Rose?

Could she ever trust Ramsey?

She'd have to worry about all that later, she realized, knowing she'd never convince Ramsey of her innocence without taking him back to the warehouse and showing him what Frank Bonner had orchestrated.

She would convince him, though, come hell or high water. She only had to think of his kisses, of the way he made her feel, to realize she wasn't willing to give up on him, no matter how completely he'd misjudged her.

Sighing, Rose pushed her tangled hair out of her eyes and unlatched the safety belt. It was all such a mess.

And she'd thought last Monday was bad . . .

She opened the door, shielded her eyes against the glare of the morning sun and looked around for Ramsey. He was close by. She sensed him, felt herself drawn to him like filings to a magnet. He'd affected her that way from the very first.

There'd been a gut-level awareness of him she could neither explain or deny. An awareness she could only accept.

That alone should tell her something.

Right now, it told Rose he was watching her. Watching and waiting.

Slowly, she raised her eyes and looked up into the passenger side window of the diesel.

Directly into the barrel of a gun. A deadly looking revolver, dark, threatening, a steel eye sighted unerringly on her face, tightly held in the bloodstained hands of a very, very angry man.

12

'Dammit! put that gun down, Michael Ramsey. You've got a lot of nerve, pointing that thing at me after all I've gone through for you.' Rose faced him boldly, head thrown back, jaw clenched in anger, both hands on her hips.

She was magnificent. Boot-clad feet planted firmly on the rough ground, tight fitting jeans molding every curve and the desert wind whipping her long dark hair across her face and over her shoulders like a silken banner.

For one brief second Ramsey wasn't sure whether he wanted to shoot her or make love to her.

He put the gun down.

'*You've* gone through?' he bellowed, throwing the door open and leaping to the ground to confront her. 'You? I know exactly what you've gone through. A hijacking. You hijacked my truck! You left me tied up in the damned desert with bugs crawling all over me and took off with your crooked boyfriend.' He stopped directly in front of her, close enough to force her to look up to see his face. He expected Rose to back down.

She didn't.

'You lied to me.' She telegraphed anger with every word. 'First of all, get this straight. I am not, let me repeat, not one of the hijackers. That was all your idea. You suspected me, you set me up, from the very beginning. You were so ready to believe I was guilty, you never even considered my innocence. But the worst thing of all . . . worst of all . . . ' She clamped her mouth shut and turned away.

'Worst of all what, Rose?' Ramsey growled.

'Nothing.'

'Rose?'

'Worst of all, you asked me to trust you, but you didn't trust me,' she whispered. 'You said you cared about me, that you'd never hurt me.'

'So I made a mistake,' Ramsey growled, unwilling to believe he could have been so wrong. 'It won't happen again. Kathleen, you got your cuffs? The two who tied me up referred to her as their boss. I don't want to take any chances until we get this sorted out.'

'Are you sure, Ramsey?' Kathleen hopped down from her hiding place against the back of the diesel and stuffed her automatic pistol into a shoulder holster hidden beneath her vest. Rose whirled around to get her first look at Ramsey's partner.

She was as tall as Rose, dressed all in black from her high heeled leather boots and tight stretch jeans to her shiny silk blouse and leather vest. Her blond hair whipped about her shoulders in the stiff breeze and except for the massive bruise on her face and badly swollen eye, she was devastatingly beautiful. And thankfully, very much alive.

'I was so worried about you.' Rose took a step toward Kathleen. 'Frank Bonner, Acme's president, wanted you dead. The man who knocked you out said he was certain he'd killed you.'

'I'm too hard headed for that, Ms. DeAngelo. It's a pleasure to finally meet you. And no, Ramsey, I do not intend to cuff her.' She smiled at Rose and any jealousy Rose had felt over the woman's relationship with Ramsey fled. How could she be jealous of someone as open and forthright as this?

'I'm Kathleen Malone,' the woman said, holding her hand out. 'My friends,' she glared at Ramsey out of the corner of her unswollen left eye, 'call me Kat.'

Rose returned her firm handshake. She liked Ramsey's partner immediately. This woman would believe her. 'Ms. Malone . . . ' Rose glanced at Ramsey, at the implacable scowl on his face and took a deep breath, forcing the desperation out of her voice.

'Kat. I came back here to protect Ramsey. Acme's president, Frank Bonner, has a warehouse filled with stolen equipment south of here, near Yerington. He's planning to move everything out this morning, in fact he might already be gone. You have to believe me, I am not involved in the thefts. James Dearborn helped me escape so that I could get back and untie Ramsey before Bonner's hired killer got to him first. We need to get back to the warehouse. If we hurry, we might be able to catch them.'

'Why should we believe you' Ramsey stepped up behind Rose. 'I certainly haven't seen any hired killer. As far as I know, you're part of this gang. She could be trying to lead us off,' he added, addressing Kathleen.

'I told you the bug on the scraper puts that piece of equipment near Yerington, which only confirms what Ms. DeAngelo is telling us. Personally, I don't think she's lying, Ramsey. From what I've learned about Bonner, I wouldn't put it past him to have set her up.' Kathleen turned back to Rose. 'Can you take us there? It would be faster than trying to triangulate the exact location with our equipment.'

'Of course.' Rose turned her back on Ramsey. She could do this, compartmentalize the pain, deny the agony of his mistrust and hatred.

Deny him. How could she have misjudged the man so badly?

Rose bit her lips, found a shred of composure and attempted to smile at Kat. 'Thank you for believing me,' she said. 'The police may already be there. I tried to convince James to contact authorities, but I'm not certain if he followed through.'

'Right,' Ramsey sneered. 'You expect me to believe that?'

Rose ignored him and almost laughed when Kathleen rolled her one good eye in disgust in Ramsey's direction. Obviously his partner knew him well. Rose was too exhausted to care how well. 'I left James at a phone booth. The thing is, he's been part of the gang all along, so he may not have made the call like he promised. We need to hurry if there's any chance of catching them.'

And clearing me, she silently added, wondering if that was even possible.

As long as Ramsey doubted her, did it even matter?

'Ramsey, get on the phone and see if anyone's reported Bonner and his gang,' Kathleen said. To Rose's surprise, Ramsey turned immediately to do his partner's bidding. 'Can we take the Mercedes?'

Kathleen asked Rose. 'I had to hot wire the sedan, and it's low on gas. You got enough fuel to get us back to Yerington?'

'Yes,' Rose sighed, thankful someone was finally taking her seriously.

A moment later Rose watched Ramsey climb down from the cab, and for the first time noticed the fresh and dried blood staining his wrists and the cuffs of his jeans. Another reason for him to hate her.

He had a grim expression on his face when he crossed over to where the two women stood. He glared at Rose a moment, then he directed his comments to Kathleen. 'They're all in custody,' he said, shaking his head. 'Every last one. Not a shot fired. Someone had already authorized a car to come out here to pick me up. The FBI's taken over the investigation. Interstate theft and at least one kidnapping they know of. Agents checked the diner parking lot looking for you and were just getting ready to put out a bulletin. I told them you were with me, to send the car back, that we'd meet them at the warehouse.'

Rose appreciated the quick grin Kathleen flashed in her direction, but it was Ramsey's angry expression that held her. 'Why'd you do it, Rose? Why did you leave me here and go along with Dearborn? Don't lie to me,' he demanded, grabbing her shoulders and shaking her before she could answer. 'Are you in with them or not?'

'I already told you I wasn't involved.' Her throat tightened around the words and she blinked away tears. He still didn't believe her!

'Then what made you choose to go with Dearborn over me?'

Ramsey's voice sounded just as tight as hers. 'They didn't give me any choice. It was all part of Bonner's plan, to convince the truck driver . . . you,' she added accusingly, 'that I was their leader. That way, you'd testify against me if it ever came to trial, backing up the paper trail that supposedly leads right to me. Only you're not a truck driver, are you? I guess that's not important though, that you've been lying to me ever since we met. Is it?' She sighed, shaking her head in frustration. 'It doesn't matter. You were very easy to convince. For some reason, I guess you wanted to believe the worst of me.' She turned away, pulling out of Ramsey's grasp, unable to say anything else without breaking down.

'That doesn't answer my question, Rose. What made you agree to go along with them?'

Remembering Tim's threats made her stomach roll, and Rose pressed her arm against her middle. 'Tim threatened to hurt you,' she whispered. 'He told me he wouldn't

240

kill you, just make you wish you were dead. Like I said, he didn't give me any choice.' She turned back to him, feeling the hot tears spilling down her cheeks. 'I did what I did to protect you. You saved my life, I saved yours. We're even now. All debts are canceled.'

Rose glared at him a moment longer, then whirled about and stalked to the car. No way was she giving Ramsey the last word.

'No they're not, Rose,' he shouted after her. 'You still owe me. You owe me big time.'

* * *

Ramsey pushed the Mercedes to its limits all the way to Yerington, but it was almost noon before they reached the warehouse. He slid the big car into a parking space near a police cruiser, avoiding the last of Bonner's men as federal agents loaded them into vans.

Two men dressed alike in dark business suits approached the Mercedes just as Ramsey shut off the ignition.

'FBI,' the shorter man said, and the two of them flipped out ID cards in unison. 'I take it you're Malone and Ramsey? I'm Agent Johnson, this is Agent O'Rourke. We'll be handling the investigation.' Agent Johnson stared over Ramsey's shoulder, and frowned

241

at Rose in the back seat. 'Are you Rose DeAngelo?'

Ramsey answered for her. 'Yeah, that's her,' he said, nodding toward Rose. She hadn't said a word all the way into town, hadn't met his eyes in the rearview mirror, hadn't blinked for all he knew.

Johnson and O'Rourke looked awfully pleased to have found her. To think he'd almost believed that cock and bull story about her innocence.

He glanced at Kathleen, but her set expression told him nothing. The FBI agents walked around to the back door and the taller man helped Rose to her feet. Neither man said a word, but their grim expressions spoke volumes. Rose looked as if she were in shock.

'You gonna be okay?' Kathleen asked, then smiled with more tenderness at Rose than Ramsey had gotten from anyone all day. 'Don't worry about a thing.'

'Thanks,' Rose said. Then she was led quietly away by the two men, one walking on either side of her.

'Whaddya think, Kat?' Ramsey watched Rose disappear into the large warehouse with the two agents.

'I think you're a jackass.' Kathleen turned her back on him. 'You're on your own, kid. I don't want to leave Rose alone with those two.'

Ramsey watched his partner as she followed Rose into the warehouse. He should have offered to go along, he'd started this investigation, for crying out loud! But what help would he be to Rose?

None at all. Absolutely none at all.

★ ★ ★

Rose wanted to smile at the bemused expression on Kathleen's face, but she was just too tired. Eight hours of interrogation would exhaust anybody. Over twenty-four hours without sleep hadn't helped either.

Agent Johnson stood up and stretched, then offered his hand to Rose. 'We can't thank you enough, Ms. DeAngelo. Convincing Dearborn to call us took a lot of courage and getting him to turn state's evidence is more than we could have hoped for. I think we'll be able to settle this case and get the convictions we want, thanks to you.'

'He's terrified of going to prison. If he testifies, will he get a lighter sentence?' she asked, feeling sorry for James in spite of herself.

'That's usually the way it works. From what we've learned, Tim Anderson and Frank

Bonner ran the show. Except for the first hijacking, Dearborn's as much a victim as you. He's still guilty, but the judge will take all the circumstances under consideration.'

'Is he gone?' Rose hadn't seen James at all.

'His mother picked him up earlier and flew him back home to Pittsburgh. We trust her to keep an eye on him. He's not going anywhere and there didn't seem to be any point in holding him. This'll probably be prosecuted in Pennsylvania, since that's where Acme Insurance is headquartered. Even though Frank Bonner is the company president, the insurance company is still the primary victim in this case. Thank you again for your cooperation. We'll be in touch.'

Rose stood up and stretched. It was almost eight o'clock. Any other Monday night she'd be home alone, watching television. Instead, she'd spent the day in this small room answering the two agents' questions. Kathleen had stayed as well, offering support and silent understanding.

Ramsey hadn't even checked to see if she was alive.

'What are you going to do now?' Kathleen asked Rose as they walked out of the office and headed across the huge warehouse. Yellow caution tape crisscrossed the entire area and dark smudges covered the surface of most of the pieces of equipment where investigators had checked for fingerprints. Abandoned tools and crates littered the building. Four men were busy reassembling Ramsey's scraper. Obviously, Mike Ramsey had managed to take care of his own interests.

Rose looked away, exhausted beyond caring. 'I'm going to sleep,' she said, placing her hand on Kathleen's arm. 'Thank you. I don't think I could have stood it, being in there all alone with those men.'

'They think you're a hero.' Kathleen smiled. 'The tall cute one . . . '

'Agent Riley O'Rourke?' Rose laughed, the first laugh she'd had all day. 'You just think he's cute because he's Irish!'

'It's a start. Anyway, I heard him talking to one of the others about putting you up for a commendation. You were very brave, Rose. You did exactly what you had to do and you got out safely. Then you went back to save Ramsey and I'm still not certain he deserved it.'

'Thanks,' Rose said, her voice roughened from the lengthy interrogation. 'I'm not so sure he did either.'

Kathleen was still chuckling when they stepped out into the early evening twilight. The Mercedes was gone, but a security man guarding the warehouse waved and walked across the parking lot to speak to them.

'Are you Agent Malone?' he asked. Kathleen nodded.

'Your partner left a couple of hours ago, asked me to give you this.' He handed a note to Kathleen with a rough map and directions to a nearby motel sketched on it. 'He said to tell you he'd get a room for you. He had to get some injuries to his wrists cleaned up. One of my men'll give you a lift.'

'Thanks,' Kathleen said, her voice as rough and exhausted sounding as Rose's. 'Share a room with me?' she asked.

'I hate to intrude.' She didn't want to cry. Not now. But he'd gone without even checking on her. Gotten Kat a room, but not Rose. His cruel indifference hurt more than anything she could have imagined.

'It's not an intrusion. After spending some quality time locked in the trunk of my car, I'd just as soon not spend the night alone. We can order in dinner, buy a bottle of wine and forget either of us knows Mike Ramsey . . . except when we put the charges on his tab.'

'Sounds better all the time.' Rose wondered if she'd stay awake long enough to get the cork out of the bottle.

The shower felt wonderful, an endless supply of hot water and cheap motel soap. Rose would have stayed even longer, but Kathleen had let her use the bathroom first and she felt guilty making the other woman wait. Kathleen still had dried blood in her hair from the night before and if the number of aspirin she'd taken throughout the day could be considered evidence, a massive headache.

Rose wrapped a big fluffy towel around herself, then realized she'd left her clothes in the truck, and the truck in the desert.

She walked out of the bathroom. The first thing she spotted was her sports bag filled with her belongings sitting in the middle of one of the two queen sized beds.

'Ramsey brought 'em by,' Kathleen said, grabbing a nightshirt out of her own bag. 'He had the diesel and my car brought back into town while we were with the agents. Ya gotta love the guy.'

'How did he know I was with you?' Rose asked, ignoring Kathleen's teasing comment. Kat couldn't possibly know how Rose felt. At this point, even Rose wasn't certain.

'I called Ramsey while you were in the shower, told him you were the hero of the day and that you were spending the night with me.'

'Did he believe you?' Rose asked.

'About spending the night or being a hero?' Kathleen laughed, then answered seriously. 'I don't know. When Ramsey closes up and tucks inside himself, there's no telling what the man's thinking. Believe me, I know.' Kathleen's sad smile spoke volumes. 'He's tired, said he wouldn't be over. Which, I guess as far as you're concerned, is just as well. Oh, almost forgot. I ordered dinner. It should be delivered in a few minutes, so you might want to get something on. Ramsey said you were partial to Chinese, so that's what I got. Chinese food and a bottle of Chardonnay wine. Hope that's okay.' She closed the bathroom door behind her.

Rose sank to the edge of the mattress, knowing her legs wouldn't hold her up any longer. How could he do this to her? Even the FBI agents agreed she was innocent, Kathleen trusted her, but Ramsey wouldn't even speak to her. Then he had the gall to tell Kathleen to order Chinese food! The man had the sensitivity of a stump.

She wanted to cry, but it would take too much effort. She wished she didn't love him, but it was too damned late for that. Instead, she dialed Aunt Rosa's number.

* ★ ★

Ramsey stared at the wall separating the two rooms and sensed Rose's nearness on the other side. 'Son of a . . . ' He threw the wet towel on the floor and dropped down onto the lumpy mattress, feeling uncharacteristically sorry for himself. He couldn't help the way he felt about Rose, couldn't change the fact loving her had made it even harder to trust her.

Ramsey thought about the tongue-lashing Kathleen had given him. Damn, but he deserved it. Rose had broken the case wide open, had convinced James Dearborn to turn state's evidence and had essentially nailed one of the nation's most wanted men. And that was before anyone realized Frank Bonner was the one they wanted. She'd been better at Ramsey's job than he had.

She'd accomplished all of it while he rolled around in the dirt, hog-tied and calling her every name in the book. He'd been so quick to blame Rose for his own failings he knew he'd never be able to face her again.

He thought about Kathleen's suggestion, that he should just admit to Rose he was the biggest jerk on the face of the earth, beg her forgiveness and ask if there was a chance for them.

The idea had merit, but it would never work.

No, Rose would be better off without him. She needed a man who understood the art of compromise, who knew what love was all about.

Even Dearborn had come through for her, risking his own life to save Rose. Ramsey had watched Dearborn leave earlier, hauled off by his harridan of a mother. He hoped the man was still on good terms with his therapist. Dearborn looked like he was going to need all the help he could get. With a mother like his, prison might be a reprieve.

He deserves it, for hurting Rose. But hadn't Ramsey hurt Rose even more? He closed his eyes in self-loathing. She'd never forgive him. He didn't deserve forgiveness. Rose knew the truth. He *had* set her up. Even worse, he hadn't questioned her guilt. He'd believed Tim Anderson, a sadistic thief, rather than trust the woman he loved. Pretty despicable behavior on his part.

In the morning, he'd check with Kathleen, then head on to Sacramento. It would be easier on all of them if he didn't see Rose again. He didn't need to be reminded of what he'd lost through his own pigheaded stupidity, nor remind her of what they'd shared.

Muted laughter carried through the thin

250

walls from the room next to his. Rose and Kathleen. Just his luck, the two women in his life would bond like long lost sisters. The thought of the stories Kathleen could tell Rose was enough to curdle his blood.

Before long, though, the voices died down until there was only silence next door. Exhaustion made its claim on him, as well. Yawning, Ramsey staggered into the bathroom for a much needed shower.

He stripped his clothes off and sagged against the tile wall, giving himself up to the warm spray. He'd stopped by a small clinic earlier in the afternoon where they'd cleaned the rope burns on his wrists and ankles, but the warm water reopened a few of the deeper cuts. He stared at the bloodstained water, a pink whirlpool swirling down the drain. His thoughts whirled just as quickly. So many mistakes, so many details. So many loose ends to tie up. He didn't want anything getting in the way of an early start in the morning.

Agent O'Rourke had promised the scraper would be loaded and ready to haul by nine. Ramsey appreciated the man's help in getting the equipment released, especially since it could have been held as evidence.

Thankfully, O'Rourke had understood the importance of Ramsey actually completing this job for Hannibal Trucking. The business couldn't afford any more financial setbacks. Thank goodness the buyer had been reasonable about another delay.

He'd called Handy, let him know what was going on and had taken the tongue lashing his stepfather gave him in the spirit in which it was intended. At least somebody loved him.

He'd checked on Rose, made sure Kathleen would keep an eye on her. Listened to Kathleen tell him in twenty different ways how badly he'd blown it with the woman he loved. In turn, he'd told Kathleen she was too old to spend her time unconscious in the trunk of her car over a stupid criminal case. She'd agreed with him and he'd agreed with her, something that rarely happened. Ramsey turned his face up to the stinging spray, chuckling to himself. In her own way, Kathleen had let him know she cared about him, the same as he did about her.

Most important, she'd promised to deliver Rose to Jackson, and to the safety of her Aunt Rosa's Honeysuckle Inn. Ramsey still wasn't certain the old woman existed, but that wasn't his problem anymore. At least it took him out of the loop and out of any further contact with Rose. In his current state, he knew he couldn't speak to her without breaking down. Continuing the trip to

California with Rose sitting next to him was inconceivable.

The women would take the Mercedes. Alicia Dearborn had actually been the one to suggest Rose keep James's car. Either the old lady had a heart, or she just didn't like the idea of owing Rose anything. The agency would pick up Kathleen's car at the shop where she'd left it in Wells and Ramsey had already sent the rental back.

Everything tied up, all neat and tidy.

Ramsey rinsed the soap off his body, dried himself off, bandaged his wrists, and stumbled into bed. He immediately thought of Rose, sleeping just on the other side of the wall from him.

She could have been in his bed, her long legs wrapped around his waist, her body taking him deep inside, taking him home. When he'd kissed her, tasted her tender lips, he'd seen the love in her eyes, felt it in her kiss, in her response to his touch.

He could have had Rose beside him forever.

Coulda, woulda, shoulda . . . Wasn't that what Handy used to say when Ramsey'd tried to make excuses for stupid behavior?

Well, the way he'd behaved around Rose was about as stupid as could be. He'd been so quick to believe only the worst. He'd called her a liar, accused her of contemptible things, and refused to believe her when she said she only wanted to protect him.

Even when he knew it was true. If anyone had acted contemptibly . . . Damn, he only had himself to blame. To come so close to love, to actually feel it blossoming, growing . . . too late now.

So many things he could have done, so much he should have said.

Filled with regret, he drifted into an uneasy sleep.

She came to him in his dreams, clad only in the thick fall of sable hair that framed her face and curled about her full breasts, across her wide shoulders.

He reached for her, knowing this was a dream, accepting on some level of his subconscious mind this was the only way he would ever have her. Her touch was liquid fire, her lips sweeter than honey, the ambrosia of illusion and fantasy.

Ramsey pulled her atop him, feeling her heat, the strength of her long thighs grasping his hips as she moved in a slow, languorous dance against him. He touched her face, her wide, full lips, the silken flesh beneath her breasts. His thumbs traced the dark areola, rose colored in the half light of morning. He felt the flesh quicken at his touch, the smooth texture now pebbly and taut, and his breath quickened as well.

He wrapped the long strands of her hair in his fist and pulled her face back down to his, needing the touch and taste of her mouth as much as he needed the air in his lungs.

But when her lips met his, she spoke against his mouth.

'You lied to me Ramsey . . . lied to me.'

She faded then, her image disappearing even before the sensation of touch, so that he felt her straddling his waist, felt the molten heat at her core, and held only stardust in his hands.

Don't give up, Ramsey, or you're a bigger fool than I thought. Whether you deserve it or not, she loves you.

Sweating, Ramsey lurched upright in bed. Pale light filtered between the heavy curtains and he dragged huge gulps of air into his lungs.

'Who's there?' He looked around the room, then shook his head to clear the cobwebs from his brain. Obviously no one. Even the stardust was gone. In its wake he felt a sense of loss and despair unlike any he'd ever known.

But the voice . . . the voice had been strangely familiar, the raspy, scratchy, irritating voice reminding him just how big a fool he was.

As if he didn't already know.

'I don't need somebody telling me what a jerk I am on top of everything else,' he muttered, swinging his feet over the side of the bed. He recalled the dream in vivid detail and immediately regretted his active imagination. That damned unfulfilled fantasy had left him in enough pain already.

No better than you deserve.

'What?' Not only was he participating in lifelike fantasies, he was definitely hearing voices. Voices? *Not just any voice — a particular voice. A voice that sound's just like Carol Channing.*

Shaking sleep from his befuddled mind, Ramsey headed for the shower. What was it Rose had said about the mysterious Aunt Rosa? Something about living with a cross between Auntie Mame and Dolly Levi?

'Nah,' he muttered as he turned on the spigots. 'I don't think so.'

13

Yerington, Nevada. Tuesday morning

A light tap sounded against the half open door to Ramsey's motel room. He glanced at his watch, then raised his head and muttered a terse greeting to the uniformed police officer standing just outside. Eight-thirty on the nose. Exactly as O'Rourke had promised.

'Mr. Ramsey? I'm your ride to the warehouse. Agent O'Rourke couldn't get away this morning.'

'Thanks. I'm about ready.' Ramsey zipped the sports bag shut and checked one last time around the room to see if he'd left anything. Except for the unmade bed and the pile of wet towels on the bathroom floor, the place was as empty and soulless as any other motel room.

He'd said a terse good-bye to Kathleen over an hour ago, knocking quietly on her door to let her know his plans. The disappointment in her eyes had been a painful thing to see.

Almost as painful as his brief glimpse of Rose, sound asleep in the bed across the room. Kathleen had moved quickly to block his view, had promised to watch out for Rose, then shut the door in his face.

The glare she'd given him said it all.

She'd called him a coward last night.

She was right.

She'd accused him of breaking Rose's heart.

Right again.

She'd said he didn't have the slightest idea what love was all about.

He had her there. Ramsey knew he'd learned a lot about love over the past few days, the love of a man for a woman, the love between friends. He'd even glimpsed the promise of love between a father and child when he'd turned the budding delinquent over to his father, and again when he'd held tiny Victoria Rose in his arms.

Most of all, he'd learned it wasn't for him, no matter how much he wanted it. The night before, he'd tried to explain his feelings to Kathleen and she'd just laughed. Why couldn't she understand how he'd failed?

Maybe it was funny, Ramsey thought as he closed the door and followed the officer across the lot to the patrol car. Kathleen said he didn't understand love, when he was doing the most loving thing he could for Rose.

He was walking out of her life. Setting her

free. Someday she'd thank him. Maybe she'd even laugh about it, laugh about the misguided investigator who thought she was a crook. That was a story for the grandkids.

There'd been one brief moment where he'd actually thought it could be a story to tell their grandkids.

Against his will, Ramsey glanced toward Rose and Kathleen's room. The Mercedes was gone. He had to swallow twice to get past the big lump in his throat when he realized they hadn't even said good-bye.

Not that he wanted them to. He'd already said his goodbyes to Kathleen. It merely surprised him Rose was gone and he hadn't even known she'd left. That was all.

Except it left him without closure, without a sense of having ended what had never really begun. For that, they would need to talk.

Well, there was always the telephone.

He really should call Rose. He had an obligation to her as much as to himself if either one of them ever wanted to get beyond what had happened this past week.

A perfectly logical reason to get in touch with Rose. Yeah, he really needed to call Rose. And soon. Definitely soon. He'd do it. Whistling tunelessly, Ramsey climbed into the patrol car and fastened his seat belt.

'Are you sure I'm doing the right thing?' Rose reached for the door handle, then turned back to Kathleen.

'I'm sure. Look, the man is hard-headed, obtuse and stubborn as a mule, but he loves you more than life itself. He wouldn't be so upset by all this if he didn't. Trust me Rose, I know Mike Ramsey better than his own mother. You can't work stake-outs and long term investigations with a guy for as many years as I have and not know more about him than you should.'

She laughed, then squeezed Rose's hand. 'If you want him, you're going to have to fight for him. But remember, the one you're going to have to fight the hardest is Michael Ramsey. Convince him he can't live without you, but don't do it unless you're certain you can't live without him. He's a good man and he doesn't deserve any less.'

'My aunt said essentially the same thing.' Rose smiled, remembering the conversation. 'I called her last night. I needed a dose of her common sense and what I got was more matchmaking.'

'You mean there really is an Aunt Rosa? Ramsey and I thought maybe you made her up, just to keep him on his toes.'

'Why would I do that? You must think I'm a complete nut if you believe I've got an imaginary aunt. Whatever made you come to that conclusion?'

Kathleen frowned in concentration, then grinned. 'It was the other night, in Salt Lake, when you said you'd talked to your aunt. We had your phone tapped and it didn't . . . ' A look of consternation crossed Kathleen's face. 'I guess you didn't know, did you?'

'You and Ramsey tapped my phone?'

'I'm sorry.' Kathleen rested her hand on Rose's shoulder. Rose twisted away, sickened by an overwhelming sense of violation and betrayal. She took a deep breath, then another. Kathleen had merely been doing her job. Rose shouldn't fault her for following orders.

Ramsey's orders.

She knew he'd suspected her from the time he changed the route, she'd just never considered the extent to which he had gone to find her guilty. Somehow, in the back of her mind, she had pictured Ramsey crusading to prove her innocence.

Her knight in shining armor, coming to his damsel's rescue once again.

Instead, he'd been trying to prove her guilt.

'How long did he suspect me? When did he first think I was involved?'

Kathleen looked down at the ground, then across the parking lot, finally back at Rose. 'Before he ever knew you,' she said.

'No.' Rose swallowed, the sour taste of bile heavy in her throat. *From the very beginning?*

'He had access to your files as part of the investigation. We know now that he was reading information Frank Bonner fed him. Your boss is a pro, Rose. He set you up. Ramsey had no reason to disbelieve what he saw in the records. When he realized he'd just pulled Rose DeAngelo out of a burning car, he figured the Fates were handing you to him on a silver platter. We maintained contact, expecting you to slip, somehow, but you didn't. The more he got to know you, the less Ramsey wanted to think you were involved, but every lead pointed in your direction. I knew right away Ramsey hoped you were innocent. He . . . '

'The route change? Tim Anderson mentioned . . . ' Rose watched Kathleen's eyes flicker away, then back to hers. There was resignation in her voice when she answered.

'Planned to see who you contacted. Even Ramsey's stepdad didn't know what route he was taking. You were the only one.'

'What's his stepfather got to do with it?' Did it even matter anymore? She thought of all of Ramsey's words of trust and wondered if she'd ever trust anyone again.

'You know Handy and his big mouth,' Kathleen was saying. Rose suddenly felt as if she might faint. Kat's voice sounded far, far away. 'He would have told someone, ruined the whole thing.'

'Handy Hannibal? He's Ramsey's stepfather?'

'I thought you knew,' Kathleen said. 'Handy married Ramsey's mom when Ramsey was about twelve. I figured you knew. I don't know why he didn't tell you the truth about their relationship. Honestly I don't.'

'That's simple,' Rose said, her voice dull and lifeless even to her own ears. 'Handy's so proud of his son, he brags about him to everyone he meets. I've heard all about Michael, the famous investigator, how important he is. Guess I should have asked what it was Michael investigated. If I'd known Ramsey was Handy's son, I would have put two and two together.'

And maybe none of this would have happened.

'I'm sorry Rose. He should have been the one to tell you all this. He would have, given the chance.' Kathleen's blue eyes filled with tears. 'Will you do that? Give him a chance?'

'Don't you understand?' Rose clutched both of Kathleen's hands in hers. 'The way I feel about him, it's all been honest. I fell in love with a truck driver who saved my life, not an investigator who had me pegged as his prime suspect. I'm in love with a man who doesn't exist!'

'Think about what you just said, Rose. Were you really completely honest? You told me last night you suspected Ramsey might be one of the crooks. You even went through his pockets, would have checked his wallet if you'd had the chance. That may not be the same as tapping a phone, but it doesn't show a whole lot of trust, either.'

Rose flushed and bowed her head, dismayed by Kathleen's perceptive, but gentle reproof.

'You fell in love with Mike Ramsey,' Kathleen said, squeezing Rose's hands. 'It doesn't matter if he's a truck driver or a DOT investigator. What matters is that you love him. And he loves you.'

Rose pulled away from Kathleen's compassionate grasp, then wrapped her arms around her middle. She bowed her head, sighing in mute frustration.

Things were never going to be the same. *But isn't that what you wanted?* a voice in her mind asked. She could have sworn it sounded like her aunt, right down to the 'I told you so,' inflection. Of course, for some convoluted reason, Aunt Rosa was convinced that Mike Ramsey, and only Mike Ramsey, was the perfect man for Rose . . . and she hadn't even met him.

If she didn't feel so much like crying, Rose was afraid she'd start laughing.

She'd asked God for help, He'd sent a bolt of lightening, a burning tree and Mike Ramsey to her rescue. She'd called her aunt for advice and Aunt Rosa had given it in no uncertain terms.

Who was Rose DeAngelo, to think she could fight the combined forces of God and Aunt Rosa?

'Rose?' Kathleen's voice was filled with concern.

Rose sighed, raised her head and took another deep breath. 'I can't believe I still love the jerk,' she whispered. 'Damn.'

'You do? Really?' Kathleen laughed, then threw her arms around Rose and hugged her. 'I'm so sorry,' she said, laughing even harder.

'It's all your fault, you and my aunt,' Rose said, pulling away from Kathleen and wiping tears from her eyes. 'When I talked to her last night she told me not to expect love to fall into my lap. She said if he's not worth fighting for, he's not worth loving. I'm still thinking that one over. And by the way, I called her from a pay phone at the motel in

Salt Lake, which is probably why your bug didn't copy.' She tried to laugh, but instead, she sighed, emotionally exhausted, physically shaken to realize how badly she wanted Ramsey, in spite of himself.

But Aunt Rosa's advice went both ways. Mike Ramsey owed Rose DeAngelo some answers. And an apology. A very sincere apology. She straightened her shoulders. 'Do you honestly think we have a chance?' she asked Kathleen.

'Yeah, I do. He'll come around. Especially once he's seen you in that red silk blouse of mine. That is one hot number, lady.' She laughed, then just as suddenly her expression sobered. 'I think you're ready to forgive him, Rose. The hard part's going to be getting him to forgive himself.' She shook her head slowly from side to side. 'Ain't love fun?' she teased, breaking into a wide smile.

'Right,' Rose answered sarcastically. 'I guess I just never expected it to be so much work.'

'That's probably why I haven't got a husband. I've spent so much time with Ramsey, I decided it wasn't worth the effort.'

'Ms. Malone? I've been looking for you.' Agent Riley O'Rourke strode across the parking lot, his dark hair shining blue-black in the morning sunlight. 'I thought you might want to go over my report, make certain I didn't leave anything out,' he said, acknowledging Rose with the nod of his head. She grinned at the suddenly smitten look on Kathleen's face as the tall blonde looked up into the twinkling blue eyes of the much taller agent.

'Of course,' Kathleen said, 'whatever you want.'

'I'll hold you to that.' O'Rourke laughed, a full-throated, infectious sound. 'Now?'

'Of course,' Kathleen repeated, a bemused expression on her face. 'Whatever you want.'

'Remember what you were saying about effort, Kat?' Chuckling, Rose hugged her friend. 'Luck to you,' she said, turning around and climbing back into the cab of Ramsey's truck.

'And to you. I'll make sure Dearborn's mother gets her car back. You take care.' Kathleen grabbed Agent O'Rourke's arm and the two of them headed in the direction of the warehouse. 'I'm gonna phone you next week,' she called out, walking backwards while still holding onto the agent's arm. 'I don't want to miss the wedding.'

'Right,' Rose muttered, curling up in her familiar corner in the front seat of Ramsey's diesel truck. She felt as if she'd come home, that she belonged here. It remained to be seen how Ramsey would feel.

'Thanks for the ride.' Ramsey climbed out of the patrol car and stretched, then grabbed his overnight bag. The truck and trailer were parked alongside the warehouse, the scraper already loaded and tied down. He saw Agent Johnson and waved to get the man's attention.

'Any more papers to sign before I take my rig?'

'No, I think we've got everything in order. Your partner's checked over the reports and I'll mail a copy to your office in about a week. You'll be kept abreast of the investigation. We'll need your deposition, but not for awhile.'

'Thank you.' Ramsey shook the man's hand. 'Tell your partner I appreciate the way both of you handled Ms. DeAngelo. You could have been pretty rough on her. Kathleen said you made it as easy an experience as you possibly could.'

'Interrogating a witness is never easy, but Ms. DeAngelo is quite a gal,' Johnson said, giving Ramsey an appraising look. He suddenly felt like a bug under a microscope. 'She had nothing but praise for you, you know.'

'No, I didn't know,' Ramsey muttered,

ashamed. No wonder Kat had read him the riot act.

'Well, I thought you should.' Johnson straightened, suddenly all business. 'Give us a call when you get back to your office and we'll clear up the details.'

'Of course.' Ramsey walked over to the rig and checked the tie downs. He circled the trailer twice, making certain the scraper was firmly in place and the trailer and lights properly hooked up.

He checked his watch. Almost ten after nine. If he drove straight through, he should be able to make Sacramento in under five hours. It wouldn't be the same, though, traveling without Rose. Nothing would ever be the same again. Sighing, Ramsey climbed up on the step, opened the door and stopped in his tracks.

He'd started the day hearing voices. Why should he be surprised by more hallucinations?

'I can't believe, after all we've been through, you were just going to go off and leave me.'

Angry hallucinations. 'Rose? What are . . .'

'I am fed up to here,' she said, swiping one long finger across her beautiful throat, 'with men running my life and lying to me. Men saying things they don't really mean and making promises they never intended to keep. Well, you promised me a ride to California and by golly I want it.'

Ramsey took a deep breath, then another, wondering if he was going to hyperventilate. Not in his wildest dreams, and they'd been pretty wild, had he imagined Rose sitting up here in the cab, glaring at him with fire in her eyes, looking pretty as a picture in tight black jeans and a red silk blouse.

Ready to go to California. With him. Even though he'd treated her like the worst criminal, had lied to her, had planned to disappear out of her life without a trace, she still wanted to be with him. The woman must have a loose screw, but he could live with that. She'd need a few loose screws to put up with him. He fumbled with his keys.

'Are we going or not?' she demanded.

'We're going.' He slid behind the wheel, turned the key and hit the starter. 'Do you want to explain . . . '

'I don't want to explain anything,' she said, speaking louder to make herself heard over the roar of the engine. 'I don't even particularly want to talk to you,' she added, not pausing to draw a breath. 'Because if I talk to you, then you'll probably talk back, and how will I know if you're telling me the truth? Men,' she huffed, sitting back in her seat.

'Rose . . . '

'Don't you 'Rose' me. You had my phone tapped. I can't believe you did that! You suspected me even before you saved my life, didn't you?' Before he could answer, she drew a deep breath and continued. 'If I didn't know it was beyond even your devious machinations, I'd think you planned the lightning bolt and the car wreck just so I'd feel indebted to you! How could you save my life and be so damned heroic and make me fall in love with you and still be such a jerk?'

'Rose, I'm really sorry . . . ' She loved him? Ramsey felt the first true stirrings of hope. Maybe once she got all this off her chest . . .

'Sorry won't cut it, Ramsey.' She twisted around, facing him as much as the seatbelt would allow. The silk blouse, unbuttoned to show the dark hollow between her breasts, rose and fell with each breath and her eyes flashed green fire.

Passion simmered behind every word she spoke, reminding Ramsey of the anger he'd felt toward Rose that night in the desert. He realized with sudden insight, their anger was as passionate and powerful as their love.

It was definitely an intriguing concept, but one he wasn't certain Rose was in the mood to appreciate. He grinned at her, then glanced down at the deep cleavage visible beneath the blood red silk. 'Nice blouse,' he said, appreciating the view even more when she took a harsh, angry breath.

'We're not talking blouses, here, Ramsey. Besides, I'm sure you've seen it before. Your partner gave it to me. You know, the woman who tapped my phone? At your request, I might add.' She glared at him.

'Remember all that talk about honesty? Sometimes, Ramsey, I wonder if you've been honest with me at all. You said you cared about me, but you were lying. If you really cared, you would have wanted to believe I was innocent. You wouldn't have listened to a single thing Tim Anderson said about me. You would have trusted me.'

She chewed thoughtfully on her upper lip, then sighed. Her shoulders appeared to sag with either defeat or exhaustion. 'This was a big mistake,' she said, staring down at her hands clenched tightly in her lap. 'I shouldn't be here.'

'Why are you?' Ramsey asked, afraid of what her answer might be. 'Here, I mean. With me.'

'Kat . . . my aunt. They told me I shouldn't give up on you,' she said with her usual bluntness.

'Have you?'

'What?'

'Given up on me?' He held his breath.

Rose sighed again, a whisper of defeat that filled the air around them. 'I don't know, Ramsey. Should I?'

He wanted to shout, *No, don't give up, not now.* Except he couldn't do that to her. What did he have to offer Rose? A man so dysfunctional he still couldn't tell her how much he loved her. A man with a job that kept him on the road most of the year, often for weeks at a time. What kind of life could he give her?

'Maybe you should,' he said, turning away from the stricken look in her eyes. 'There's always going to be anger, Rose. Do you really think you'll ever forgive me for mistrusting you? That's baggage you'll carry around forever. Not a good way to start a marriage.'

'Marriage, Ramsey? Who said anything about marriage?'

'Isn't that what you're talking about?'

'Absolutely not.' She stared at him with guileless green eyes. 'You don't actually think I'd want to marry you after the way you've treated me, do you? Good Lord, Ramsey, you were all ready to handcuff me, even when you knew I was innocent!'

'I didn't know for sure,' he insisted,

downshifting as the big rig headed up a steep grade.

'Well, you should have believed me. I don't lie,' she added indignantly.

'Yes you do,' he said. 'You're not very good at it, but you lied to me.'

'When?' She snorted the word.

'You lied about the phone call to Dearborn. You insisted you hadn't been on the phone.'

'That phone call was private. Which reminds me, how did you know I talked to James? Were you tapping my phone then, too?'

'No. Kat checked the phone records. We traced the call to Dearborn's home.'

Rose's green eyes glittered with angry heat, but her voice was cold as ice. 'Is there any other snooping you did that you might want to tell me about?'

'Not any I can think of.' Ramsey gritted his teeth. The woman was absolutely impossible!

'Well, if you think of anything else, let me know, will you?' Rose glared at him, folded her arms across her chest and turned away.

Ramsey took a deep, calming breath, and let the air out in a low whistle between his teeth. He glanced at Rose, then back along the ribbon of highway leading them to Sacramento.

At this rate, it looked like it was going to be a long, cold ride to California.

But Rose is beside me.

Ramsey wondered if she'd given up on him yet.

They stopped briefly in Truckee for a sandwich, but the conversation between them was brief and stilted. Ramsey figured he had his answer. He'd thought about it all the way over the Sierra Nevada mountains. Rose may have climbed back into his truck of her own free will, but it was obvious, as much as she might want to forgive him, she'd never be able to forget.

He'd only been doing his job. He hadn't meant to fall in love, especially with a woman who, even though she thought she loved him, would always view him with suspicion and mistrust. What kind of future would that be, for either one of them?

His first decision had been the right one.

He'd deliver Rose to her aunt's, then leave.

He owed her that much.

And it would make things so much easier. She wouldn't have to give up on him, he wouldn't force her to make that choice.

He'd just tell her he'd given up on her.

14

Ramsey barely said a word as they wound down out of the mountains. Every so often Rose glanced in his direction, but he had shut her out completely. An ache settled deep in her middle, a painful sense of desolation and loss.

She'd given it her best shot, but she knew she'd failed. She'd tried to do everything Aunt Rosa and Kathleen had suggested. She'd put her heart on the line the minute she climbed into Ramsey's truck, but she hadn't been able to contain the anger she still felt.

She could have kept her mouth shut, but what would that prove? If they couldn't have trust, couldn't be honest with each other about their feelings . . .

Maybe he was right. Maybe she'd never be able to shed the feelings of betrayal and mistrust, never get beyond the lies they'd both been guilty of. Sighing, Rose settled back against the warm leather seat.

Kathleen had said the hard part would be getting Ramsey to forgive himself.

For what? For doing his job? Rose bowed

her head with the shameful realization she hadn't given him a chance. She still blamed him for doing what he'd been hired to do.

To catch a thief. Was it really Ramsey's fault all the evidence, including Rose's unwitting behavior, had turned her into the prime suspect?

Absolutely not. She and Ramsey were both victims of Frank Bonner's manipulations. She'd been unfair to blame Ramsey for doing exactly what he'd been paid to do.

On the other hand, was it his fault she'd fallen in love?

Yes, dammit! If he hadn't been exactly what he was, hard-headed and brave, compassionate and determined, funny, loyal and stubborn as a mule, she wouldn't love him the way she did.

A lot of good it's gonna do you. Rose glanced at Ramsey's implacable profile, the stern line of his jaw and the rigid set of his shoulders, and silently admitted to herself it was too late. He'd asked her to trust him and she'd failed miserably.

The dark green mountain forest gave way to rolling hills and grassland as they sped toward California's Central Valley. Tension, thick and silent, filled the diesel cab by the time they finally pulled into the outskirts of Sacramento around two in the afternoon.

By four, Ramsey had transferred the equipment to its new owner, contacted his agency, called Kathleen and rented a car. Suddenly, they were on the road once again, heading back up into the Sierra Nevada foothills toward the small community of Jackson.

Rose hardly noticed the rainbow of spring colors, the wide fields of blue lupine and the masses of golden poppies covering the hillsides. How could she, with Ramsey so close beside her in the small rental car their shoulders nearly touched?

'How much farther is it?' Ramsey asked. Rose didn't need psychic abilities to sense his impatience. He couldn't wait to be rid of her. She'd hoped, oh how she'd hoped there might be a chance for the two of them. Kathleen was certain Ramsey loved her, even Aunt Rosa had encouraged Rose to throw caution to the wind, to take a chance on love.

Well, for once, it looked like her aunt just might be wrong.

Rose buried the sharp stab of pain, and forced herself to think about the Honeysuckle Inn. She could almost smell the sweet perfume of the flowers. Once she got home, she'd be able to handle anything.

Even Ramsey's leaving.

'Only a few miles. I hope Aunt Rosa's back

when we get there. When I talked to her last night, she said she'd be gone most of the day. I was hoping you'd get a chance to meet her ... I mean, since I've talked about her so much. You're probably pretty tired of hearing all my Aunt Rosa stories.'

Ramsey grunted his acknowledgment. Rose looked away, embarrassed to realize she'd been babbling. The tension in the small car seemed to magnify her words, make everything sound stupid and inane. She chewed on her upper lip and wished the miles away.

'Turn here.' She pointed to a smaller road off to the left. They followed its meandering path for a couple of miles, clattering over cattle guards and fording tiny streams. At one point they stopped for a herd of sheep. The animals took their own sweet time crossing the road, despite the combined efforts of a shepherd and his well-trained border collie.

Just ahead, a gnarled and twisted oak tree spread its branches completely across the road. 'At the big oak,' Rose said, unable to contain her excitement. It had been a long two years. Almost as long as the last hundred miles. 'That driveway beside it. See the sign? Stop, please?'

Ramsey pulled through the open gate and parked beneath the beautiful hand-lettered sign hanging overhead. He glanced at Rose, at the tears sparkling in her eyes and it was all he could do not to pull her into his arms. Instead, he turned away and stepped out of the car. Rose got out as well. She stood by the open door on the passenger side, her face turned slightly away so that he saw her only in profile.

The Honeysuckle Inn sat on a small knoll at the end of a long, curving driveway, so perfectly designed it appeared to flow out of the brilliant green lawn beneath it. The farmhouse reminded Ramsey of the set of an old John Wayne western, but the cream colored paint glistened and the dark green shutters matched the color of Rose's eyes.

A wide porch covered in honeysuckle surrounded the stately old home and Ramsey finally understood Rose's love for the inn. Masses of flowers hung heavy and sweet, their fragrance saturating the air and lulling the senses. The massive vine twisted and trailed along the porch, twining between the railings and up over the eaves.

Ramsey inhaled the sweet perfume, drawing it deep into his lungs. For a moment time stood still as he absorbed the essence of Rose's childhood.

Rose took a shuddering breath and climbed back into the car, slamming the door and breaking the spell.

Ramsey got in and drove up to the front of the inn. Rose glanced at him, tears spilling over her cheeks. 'Thanks for bringing me home, Ramsey.' Her voice sounded choked with tears, filled with emotion.

'Sure,' he whispered, swallowing deeply. This had been a long journey for Rose. An even longer one for him. Had they only known each other for just over a week? It seemed impossible Rose could have become so firmly entwined in his heart in such a short time.

Her movements jerky and slow, Rose walked up the front steps. Ramsey gazed wistfully at her, then forced himself to look away. A lump filled his throat and he sat there a moment longer struggling for composure. He could have this, all of this, if only . . .

No, you can't. Not if you love her.

And that was it. She deserved better. Rose deserved trust and honesty, and a man willing to commit to her for the rest of her life. He'd already proved he wasn't that man. Bowing his head in defeat, Ramsey got out of the car and followed Rose up the stairs.

He hesitated at the top step. Standing beneath the enveloping vine, he felt intoxicated by the sweet scent of honeysuckle. Masses of white and gold flowers hung in vibrant contrast to the soft green leaves.

Hummingbirds darted in and out, oblivious to the humans standing so close.

Rose belonged here, as much a part of the inn as the vine around it. He imagined her as a child, playing beneath its fragrant shade. Then the image shifted to one of Rose sitting in the big old porch swing with a toddler at her knee and a baby at her breast.

Ramsey shook his head to clear his mind. He couldn't think clearly, not when she was this close, not when the honeysuckle filled his senses and dreams of Rose filled his heart.

'I guess Aunt Rosa's still not home,' she said, checking the front door and finding it locked. Rose lifted the top off a small birdfeeder hanging from the porch. The front door key hung inside, tied to a piece of twine. 'Everybody in town knows this is where my aunt keeps it,' she said, inserting the key. 'I sometimes wonder why she even locks the place.'

She stepped through the open door, blinking to adjust her eyes after the bright afternoon sunshine. A sense of familiarity washed over her, soothing Rose's raw nerves and anxious heart.

Nothing had changed. The big oak table in the dining room had its usual coating of dust, the one in the big, square, country kitchen looked freshly scrubbed and ready to set.

Plants filled the windows, fragrance filled the air.

Rose turned to smile at Ramsey.

He wasn't there.

Trembling, she hurried back to the entrance and looked out the front door. Ramsey stood behind the car. Rose's sports bag hung from his shoulder and as she watched, he slung her coat over his arm and shut the trunk with a loud *thunk*.

He'd left his own luggage in the car.

Her shoulders slumped in defeat as he slowly headed up the walk. She thought she'd prepared herself for the pain of losing him, but she hadn't expected this agonizing pressure forcing the air from her lungs, or the knifelike thrust to her heart. Concentrating on the act of breathing, Rose fought the spasm that turned her heart to stone.

She stepped aside when Ramsey walked through the door and set the bags on the floor. 'You're not staying, are you?' she said, amazed when her voice sounded calm and matter-of-fact.

He bowed his head a moment, then looked directly into her eyes. 'I care about you, Rose. A lot. I know you feel something for me, or you wouldn't have been out there in the truck this morning. If we'd started out differently, without all the lies between us . . . you and I know I'm not what you need. I've got my job and it keeps me on the road all the time. When this case goes to trial, I'm going to be needed for a lot of the testimony. There're so many commitments I have to deal with. I've never stayed in one place, never had a relationship, I . . . '

'Then go.' She straightened her spine and looked into the eyes of the one man she would ever love. 'I won't ask you to stay, but I'm not afraid to say the words. I love you, Michael Ramsey. And you love me, but you're too big a coward to say so. As for all those commitments ' . . . you don't know the meaning of the word. You only know excuses. I think you'd better leave.'

'I didn't plan any of this, Rose.' He clenched his fists at his sides and his eyes glistened with the hint of unshed tears. Rose wished she could just slap some sense into him.

Instead, somehow, she laughed.

'Remember what we talked about earlier, Ramsey? Life's what happens to you when you're making plans. You make excuses instead of plans When you're ready to stop making excuses and get a life, give me a call.'

She reached up with her free hand, grabbed him by the back of the neck, and pulled his face down to her level. Before he could react, she kissed him on the mouth, hard and quick, then jerked away before he could kiss her back.

If that doesn't shock some sense into you, I don't want you, she vowed, savoring the taste of him on her lips, the shell-shocked expression in his deep gray eyes.

But she did, she admitted as he silently turned and left the house. She really did want him.

★ ★ ★

She'd asked him to leave. Just like that, no strings, no tears, nothing. Nothing but a kiss that almost knocked his socks off. He could still taste her on his lips, the rich flavors of Rose that hinted at so much more. He glanced back at the inn, but she'd shut the door. He rested his forehead on the steering wheel and stuck the key in the ignition.

He couldn't quite bring himself to turn the damned thing on.

Commitments. He'd told Rose he couldn't stay because he had commitments. What could be more important than the woman he loved? Was anything more important than what he felt for Rose?

Frustrated, he sat back and pounded his fist on the steering wheel, then took a deep breath. What the hell was he trying to prove, anyway? How big a fool he could be?

What did Rose say? *Life is what happens to you when you're making plans.* He never planned, he just took assignments. One lousy job after the other.

Hard to get more foolish than that. He looked back at the inn. A sense of peace enveloped him, and he knew. The only place he was ever going to find peace was here, with Rose at his side.

Because, whether he liked it or not, he needed her every bit as much as she needed him. Only a damned fool would pass up a chance for that kind of love.

Well, he for one was tired of playing the fool.

Ramsey pulled the key out of the ignition, stuck it in his pocket, and grabbed his bag out of the back seat.

Go for it, boy! I knew you had it in you!

'What the hell?' Carol Channing giving him a bad time in a motel room dream he could understand, but she had no business offering him encouragement in the driveway of the Honeysuckle Inn!

'Aunt Rosa, where the hell are you?'

The only answer was the chattering of hummingbirds and the steady hum of bees. Ramsey stood there a moment, taking in the sounds and smells, then grinned and pocketed the keys. Rose did say her aunt claimed to be psychic.

Somehow, he had to convince Rose to give him another chance. He'd deal with Aunt Rosa later.

★ ★ ★

Rose sensed him behind her even before he kissed the nape of her neck, but she didn't turn around. She concentrated instead on the view out the kitchen window, the view she couldn't have described even if her life depended on it.

Concentrated until her will snapped with the touch of Ramsey's lips.

Rose's heart beat so fast she knew she'd never sleep again.

'Someone I love told me I should get a life.' Ramsey's words whispered and tickled against her ear. Rose trembled and hugged her arms tightly around herself.

'She was right,' she said, biting her lips to keep from giggling.

'That same someone said I needed to stop making excuses.' His breath tickled a warm caress as he gently nipped the lobe of her ear.

'And?' Rose prodded, shivering when he nibbled tiny kisses along her neck and across the ridge of her shoulder.

'I figured I'd better make myself clear.' He turned Rose around and pulled her into his arms. 'Will you forgive me, Rose? Will you take me back? Will you marry me?'

'I'll think about it.' She kissed the corner of his mouth, then stepped away before he could trap her lips with his.

'You'll think about it? What do you mean, you'll think about it?' He grabbed her around the waist, hauled her up against him, and kissed her.

She thought about struggling, thought about making him suffer the way she had when he'd walked out the door, but it was impossible to fight the power of his kiss.

Not when his lips molded hers so perfectly, not when his tongue traced the sensitive contours of her mouth, tasting and teasing with devastating thoroughness. This was Ramsey, the man she loved, the only one she wanted.

He held her, one hand entwined in her thick hair, the other molding her buttocks, kneading and rubbing the soft flesh, pressing her into the cradle of his thighs.

She felt him gloriously aroused and ready for her, his solid length hard against her belly. Her hips pressed forward, instinctively reaching for him. Moaning, she twisted her mouth away from his and dragged in huge gulps of air.

'Well?' he said, breathing just as hard.

She tried for an innocent look, she wanted to say, 'Well, what?' and couldn't. She wanted him too much for games, needed him too much to deny either of them any longer. 'I forgive you, I want you back, and yes, I'll marry you,' she blurted between panted gasps. 'But it's all off if you don't take me to bed and make love to me right now. Understood?'

'You're a hard woman, Rose DeAngelo.' He practically growled her name, but his gray eyes twinkled when he swept her up into his arms. 'Where's the bedroom?'

Laughing, she pointed to a doorway just down the hall. 'That's a guest room, but it's the closest. We'll hear if my aunt gets home.'

He kicked the door open, then kissed her, his lips a fierce promise against her mouth. 'I don't want to hear another word from your aunt. I don't want to hear anything but you. Moaning my name, asking what wonderful things you can do to my body, telling me how terrific I am. Got it?'

'Getting cocky, are we?' she asked, tugging at his hair and kicking her legs. Ramsey merely grunted his reply, kicked the door firmly shut with his foot and tossed her on the bed.

He followed her down, settling himself in the V of her thighs, holding her head immobile in his strong hands, parting her lips with his tongue and drawing her into a hot and humid world of sensation.

His hips rocked against hers, mimicking the strokes of his tongue. She arched her back and parted her thighs, pulling him even closer against her. The room, cool when they entered, now pulsed with heat and passion.

Rose tugged at Ramsey's waistband with numbed fingers, needing to touch flesh, to feel skin against skin, heat against heat. Ramsey traced the line between her breasts with his lips, his hot breath searing the red silk into her skin. She gasped her pleasure when he slowly parted the row of buttons, then carefully unhooked the clasp on the tiny wisp of a bra covering her breasts.

'Perfect,' he whispered, pushing the lacy fabric aside and cupping her delicate flesh, circling the dark nipples with his thumbs. 'I've imagined doing this ever since I watched you buy this thing.' He drew one nipple into his mouth, then the other, suckling gently at first, then increasing the pressure as the turgid buds tightened in response. Rose moaned, caught between pleasure and pain while Ramsey nibbled at the sensitive flesh.

She dragged her fingers through his hair,

holding his head to her breast, willing him not to stop.

'Ramsey.' His name slipped from between her lips, resonating with desire and love. 'Oh, God, Ramsey, I . . . '

Suddenly the rocking motion of his hips stilled. A cold rush of air flowed over her damp nipples as Ramsey slowly pulled away from her. She felt him trembling in her arms and the passionate words died on her lips. Slowly, wondering, she opened her eyes to the troubled look in his.

The chill across her naked breasts spread to encompass her entire body when Ramsey turned and swung his legs over the edge of the bed. He ran his fingers through his tangled hair, then sighed. Reaching out for Rose, he pulled her across his lap and kissed her. 'We can't do this, Rose. Not until . . . '

'Oh, no you don't, Michael Ramsey.' She pushed against his solid chest and scrambled out of his lap. 'You turn your emotions on and off faster than a light switch. You tell me you love me, you make love to me, and then you tell me . . . '

'That I'm sorry, Rose. That I have to apologize for everything I've done to hurt you. I know we've started out poorly, that we've got a lot of baggage that's gonna have to get cleared out, but when I make love to you, I only want you to think of how much I love you, not how much I've hurt you. I want a fresh start with you, and I want it to begin here, now.'

'Oh.' She looked away from his gentle smile, suddenly aware of her unbuttoned blouse draped loosely around her elbows, the cups of her lacy bra pushed back under her arms, her exposed and tingling breasts. And she admitted to herself she hadn't been blameless either.

'You were doing your job,' she said, feeling naked and vulnerable beneath his intense gaze. She glanced down at his hands resting against his powerful thighs, and saw that they trembled. 'Oh Ramsey, believe me, I understand. You did everything in your power to protect me. I know that, now.'

She heard his long, low sigh of relief, then he reached out and grasped her gently by the hips, dragging her back to him. He tugged at her blouse and bra, pulling them over her arms and tossing them to the floor. Then he proceeded to unfasten her belt and jeans and shove them to her ankles. She giggled when he couldn't tug them over her boots. She grabbed his shoulders for balance and he managed to untie her boots and slip everything off at once.

Rose stood before him, clad only in a tiny

wisp of lace barely covering her dark curls and heated center. Ramsey pulled her close, kissing and teasing her taut belly until she moaned, grinding her hips against him.

'As I was saying,' he whispered, between tiny kisses along the fragile edge of her panties, 'I am so sorry that I hurt you.' He nuzzled the tender flesh at the curve of her waist. 'But I can never be sorry for anything that brought us to this point. I love you, Rose. Once I knew you, everything I did was intended to prove your innocence.'

He slid his fingers along her slim sides, gliding over each rounded rib. 'I'm sorry I was too big a coward to admit I was wrong and I thank God you were brave enough to stick with me.'

'Bravery had nothing to do with it, Ramsey.' Her words had a breathless quality, as if she'd run a long distance. 'Like I said before, you promised me a ride to California.'

'Stubborn witch.' He spread his fingers across the soft flair of her hips and pulled her close enough to taste. Her grip on his shoulders tightened when he nibbled at her through the silken fabric that barely covered her. Then he was tugging and nipping at the fragile band encircling her hips, shredding the material until it parted and her panties fell to the floor.

Rose gasped in mock outrage, but the gasp slowly spiraled downward into an impassioned moan as he savored her, pleasuring her with teeth and tongue and lips.

He kneaded her taut buttocks, holding her shivering body against his mouth, exploring her secrets, bringing her to a peak of excitement that must rival his own. Her tiny whimpers grew breathless, her body stiffened beneath his relentless onslaught and she cried out, a harsh sound of pleasure and pain. Her fingers clenched his shoulders as her knees buckled and she dropped to his lap.

It was sweet agony to hold her, shivering and naked in his arms, to feel her pressed against him and know she belonged to him. He kissed her temple, holding his lips against her dark hair, then carefully lay her down on the bed.

Her body glistened with sweat, and her chest heaved as she dragged in huge gulps of air. She was beautiful, caught up in the aftermath of her climax. Her pleasure filled him with a sense of wonder.

★ ★ ★

Vaguely, in some peripheral part of her consciousness, Rose was aware of Ramsey settling her on the bed. She thought she heard his clothing slip to the floor, but she was too busy trying to catch her breath, trying to understand what had just happened to her to really care what he was up to.

Her body felt sensitized from one end to the other, all of her nerve endings coalescing into one melting point of heat at her center. She shivered, not from cold, but from the sudden release of energy still rippling through her.

She thought she'd known what a climax was, even thought she'd experienced one or two in the past.

She'd been wrong. Dead wrong, if the way her body felt now was any indication of what she'd been missing. A noise intruded on her numbed mind, the sound of tearing foil, a sound that made her realize just how out of touch with reality she'd been. At least Ramsey's brain must be functioning, if he was lucid enough to think about protection.

He stretched out beside her, wrapped his fingers in her hair and stroked her breasts, her torso. He touched her, gentle, featherlight strokes that made her flesh quiver in response, but she didn't open her eyes until his soft laughter dragged her out of her relaxed stupor.

He hovered over her, grinning, a wolf over its prey.

'What?' she demanded, almost petulantly. She really didn't want to lose this wonderful, replete sensation.

'You can't possibly think we're all done, can you?' he asked, bringing her body alive with the gentle strokes of his long fingers. They dipped between her legs and she was incapable of controlling her reflexive movements against them.

'I guess not,' he answered for her, then kissed her. She tasted herself on his lips and shivered again. He increased the pressure against her mouth at the same time he parted her legs and filled her. The heat built again, the delicious rush of warmth and desire from mouth to breasts to womb. She cried out again, afraid she might lose herself in the ecstasy of loving him.

Her fingers flew across his back, gliding over the sweat slick muscles, learning the planes and valleys, ridges and ripples of his body. His mouth burned against hers, drawing her deeper into the maelstrom, the rhythm of their loving punctuated by the *slap, slap, slap* of their bodies. This was no gentle coming together. He took her, possessed and loved her, filled her with his length and heat until she broke, sobbing in his arms.

He followed, gasping her name in a hoarse whisper that was as much a plea as a declaration, then collapsed on top of her, heart pounding, breath ragged. All Rose could do was hold him, wrapping her arms around his waist so he could never leave.

A moment later he rolled to his side, taking Rose with him. They lay together, touching, connected. Forever changed.

'I think I'm done now,' he said, a few minutes later. He laughed out loud, but she could only chuckle in reply. Long moments later, when his ragged breathing had finally returned to normal, he ran one finger lightly across Rose's cheek. 'You're beautiful, Rose,' he said, his voice barely above a whisper. 'Even more beautiful now, with that just loved look on your face.' He kissed her lightly on the nose.

'You guarantee these beauty treatments to last?' she asked, brushing the tangled hair back from his eyes. She loved his dark gray eyes, especially when they twinkled with love and humor. The way they were twinkling now.

'Only if continued on a regular basis.'

She trailed her fingers along his bare hip. 'How regular?' she asked, tasting one flat, brown nipple with her tongue, and feeling him grow hard once again inside her.

He grasped Rose's waist, rolled to his back,

and pulled her astride him. 'About this regular,' he said.

★ ★ ★

'It's got to be the honeysuckle.' Rose sighed audibly, and sipped at her steaming cup of coffee. 'I haven't been this relaxed in years.'

'I don't think I'd give all the credit to the honeysuckle.' Ramsey poured himself a cup of coffee and sat at the kitchen table where he could watch Rose. 'You, woman, are insatiable,' he said, trying his best to look grumpy.

Rose glanced his way and snorted, and he gave up. There was no way he'd ever wipe the silly grin off his face. Not after the night he and Rose had just spent.

Merely remembering made him hard again. He almost laughed out loud, well aware he was too damned tired to do anything about it. But there was always later . . .

The phone rang and they both jumped. Rose got up and answered it and Ramsey almost laughed aloud at the comical expressions flitting across her face. Shock, surprise, incredulous laughter and a look of utter disbelief when she finally placed the phone back in the cradle.

'That was my aunt . . . she just called to say

she eloped yesterday with her attorney and they won't be back from Reno for two days. I wondered why she didn't come home. That explains it! She's seventy-five and he's almost eighty . . . can you believe that?' She stared at him, her mouth still open in surprise.

'From what you've told me about your aunt, yes, I do believe it!' Ramsey laughed and pulled Rose down into his lap. 'Shut your mouth, Rose. You'll catch a fly.' He kissed her, and shutting her mouth was the last thing on her mind.

Awhile later they both came up for breath. 'But I haven't seen her in two years.' Rose tried her best to look indignant. It didn't work.

'Don't worry. We'll be here when they get back.' Ramsey kissed her again. 'I need to meet this aunt of yours. Somehow, I feel as if we already know each other.'

Rose wondered a moment at his cryptic smile. 'I know you'll love her,' she said. 'Aunt Rosa is really something special.'

'I can believe that,' Ramsey said, kissing Rose once again.

'I was so afraid you wouldn't come back.' Rose looped her arms over his shoulders and rested her forehead against his shoulder. 'When you went out to the car, I fully expected to hear you drive away.'

'I couldn't leave you, Rose. Not then, not

ever.' He tapped her nose with his finger as if to make a point. 'Good Lord, woman. Do you realize what we've been through together?'

A gentle breeze filtered through the open kitchen window, and filled the room with the sweet scent of honeysuckle. Rose cupped Ramsey's face in her hands and saw herself in the somber gray depths of his eyes. Though his words were meant to tease, her mind filled with the events of the week past: a little boy given a second chance with his father, a young girl finding herself in the birth of her daughter, her own harrowing escape from almost certain death . . . of choices made and roads taken. None of it planned, all of it wondrous, all of it leading to this moment with this man.

Gently, she placed her mouth against his, feeling the pressure build, the need intensify in a long, searing kiss that left both of them breathless and wanting more. 'Remember what I said about making plans?' she asked, running her fingers across his chest, slipping beneath the worn tee shirt to touch his flesh.

'You were absolutely right.' He stood up, still holding Rose in his arms, and carried her toward their room. 'I think it's time we let life happen, don't you?'

She answered him with her kiss.

We do hope that you have enjoyed reading this large print book.

Did you know that all of our titles are available for purchase?

We publish a wide range of high quality large print books including:
Romances, Mysteries, Classics
General Fiction
Non Fiction and Westerns

Special interest titles available in large print are:
The Little Oxford Dictionary
Music Book
Song Book
Hymn Book
Service Book

Also available from us courtesy of Oxford University Press:
Young Readers' Dictionary
(large print edition)
Young Readers' Thesaurus
(large print edition)

For further information or a free brochure, please contact us at:
Ulverscroft Large Print Books Ltd.,
The Green, Bradgate Road, Anstey,
Leicester, LE7 7FU, England.
Tel: (00 44) **0116 236 4325**
Fax: (00 44) **0116 234 0205**

Antique dealing has its own equivalent to 'insider trading', as Charles Ramsay finds out to his cost. Offered the purchase of a lifetime, he sees all his ambitions realised in an antique jade cup, known as the 'Loot'. But as soon as the deal is irrevocably struck he finds himself stuck with it like an albatross around his neck — unable to export it without a licence, unable to sell it at home, and in a paralysing no man's land where nobody has sufficient capital to take it off his hands . . .

NO TIME LIKE THE PRESENT

June Barraclough

Daphne Berridge, who has never married, has retired to the small Yorkshire village of Heckcliff where she grew up, intending to write the biography of an eighteenth-century woman poet. Two younger women are interested in her project: Cressida, Daphne's niece, who lives in London, and is uncertain about the direction of her life; and Judith, who keeps a shop in Heckcliff, and is a divorcee. When an old friend of Daphne falls in love with Judith, the question — as for Cressida — is marriage or independence. Then Daphne also receives a surprise proposal.

SEARCH FOR A SHADOW

Kay Christopher

On the last day of her holiday Rosemary Roberts met an intriguing American in the foyer of her London hotel. By some extraordinary coincidence, Larry Madison-Jones was due to visit the tiny Welsh village where Rosemary lived. But how much of a coincidence was Larry's erratic presence there? The moment Rosemary returned home, her life took on a subtle, though sinister edge — Larry had a secret he was not willing to share. As Rosemary was drawn deeper into a web of mysterious and suspicious occurrences, she found herself wondering if Larry really loved her — or was trying to drive her mad . . .